THE VILLAGE THAT REFUSED TO DIE
BY
SAM ALEXANDER

For Jennie

THE VILLAGE THAT REFUSED TO DIE

May 1987

Sundays generally followed a familiar pattern. I had football to play at 2pm. We weren't a good side, but we were a team made up of close friends from a small village, and we thoroughly enjoyed our Sunday afternoons, travelling the county, usually getting beaten by village sides with a lot more lads to choose from for their starting eleven's.

Dad would be up early, and in the garden, busying himself, mowing or weeding, chopping up logs, tidying the garage. He'd already cleaned my football boots, carefully polishing them with dubbing. He'd often have a gripe with me for not cleaning them after I'd got home from our match the previous Sunday.

Mum loved to cook, she'd be in the kitchen – cakes, pies, biscuits – the smell would waft through the house and tantalise our taste buds. Nan would be sat with her cup of tea in hand, a Richard Clayderman record on the stereo, chatting away about nothing-in-particular.

My sister Sasha would be in her bedroom, friend in tow. They'd be recording the Top 40 off the radio onto tape cassette. It always amazed me how good she was at pausing the song at exactly the right time to stop the dulcet tones of Bruno Brooks from interrupting her carefully planned mix tape.

It's a cliché I know but life really was much simpler back then. I don't know if that was because I was a fifteen-year-old kid with no responsibilities. My only concerns were whether mum and dad would find out that I'd not done my homework or if our VCR had recorded Match of the Day correctly. There was no social media, no 24-hour news channels, no mobile phones. The internet was yet to be invented, and the HIFI was the go-to purchase for music connoisseurs.

Our village was called Danehill, it wasn't anything special, but it was home. It was basically all situated around, and on, a gradual sloping hill. From the local primary school at the bottom to the Anglican church situated at the top. We had a pub in the middle, and a couple of village stores along with a large playing field. There was another public house on the parish outskirts, and a smattering of farms and a large estate. We had a village hall, a scout hut, and one bus stop. Nothing much ever really happened but the reason that we thrived wasn't because of the local amenities but because of a sense of community. The type that you don't get as much in the modern day.

But in the summer of 1987, in this very small and very uneventful village in East Sussex, something happened; something that would affect me and the lives of the inhabitants forever…

Wednesday June 10th

June was always a fun month in Danehill; it was a month that celebrated the anniversary of the birth of my village. And this weekend was a big one – it was the 100th birthday of our village – The Centenary Special. This was a weekend that celebrated people, art, dancing, sport, and togetherness. Everybody joined in, visitors from surrounding towns and villages came along to revel in the festivities. A huge marquee was erected on the local playing field and for four long summer days events took place to raise money for local groups and charities – to me it seemed like the whole World converged upon the parish to take part – it was the highlight of my, and many other people's year.

There were five of us, five lads. We'd all grown up in the village and had respect for the locals and the way of life was but, as kids, we were also mischievous and longed for excitement – this annual party was the perfect tonic – an excuse to lose ourselves in the hustle and bustle of what was going on around us and live our best lives. Whilst our parents readied themselves for the festivities, we would be planning our own events for the days ahead. We weren't interested in the art show or the senior citizens tea party, we had no yearning to go to the barn dance or the garden fetes, we had girls to meet and entertainment of our own to make.

There was me, Sam, football mad, and a bit of a dreamer, there was Pat, already six foot and already a lady's man. Carter lived on the same road as me, he was a deep thinker, and a mad keen sportsman and then there was Seth, a skateboarder with a penchant for reggae music. Rabbit was the elder statesman of the group – O Levels already done and soon off to college. We were a close-knit tribe and trusted each other completely.

It was on the eve of the villager's weekend that this story began. As always, a few days before a team of men arrived to erect the marquee. They would spend the days onsite and their evenings in the Alligator – the local public house. It was when they left for their evening drinking session when us local kids made the location our own. We knew that the workers would be in the pub all night and wouldn't arrive back until after eleven a little worse for wear. The younger kids would be playing huge games of hide and seek and Forty- Forty, and British Bulldog, running in and out of the scaffolding poles and bouncing about on the large cushion like seats. There would be kids on bikes utilising the builders left over apparatus to makeshift jumps. Others would be sitting round chatting on the playing field in anticipation of the good times ahead. The whole region felt alive, and it was fun to be a part of. When you are a kid, the summers seems to last forever, and in my mind, when looking back, it is always sunny. And that is exactly how I remember the beginning of that summer in 1987.

The five of us gathered on the recreation ground, football in tow. The goalposts had been taken down to make space for the marquee, so we crafted a temporary goal using jumpers as goalposts and began our familiar game of headers and volleys. As usual, the game got bigger and bigger as more and more neighbourhood kids joined in. The idea of the game was to score goals but only via a volley or a header if you missed you went in goal and if you conceded too many goals you had to put up with the ball being booted at your backside from close range. It was Pat who spent the most time in goal given his less than talented artistry with a football. Even the younger kids of the village took a turn at striking the ball at his behind and great hilarity ensued as his rear turned redder with every shot. But as the sunlight gradually faded and dwindled away, so too did many of the players and just the five of us were left.

We sat against the bank. Seth had visited the village shop earlier that evening. He was the only one with fake ID and the only one not known to the March family who ran the store. He had purchased some very weak shops-own lager, and this hit the spot as we all relaxed after our evening of sport. We all leaned back and looked out over the recreation ground, masters of our terrain – Carter and Pat lit up their cigarettes and we discussed the weekend ahead. "I'm getting paid twenty quid to help lead the car parking this year" Carter said, "If you lot want in, I can sort it". We all wanted in – money was in short supply, and we knew this was an easy job, and came with an-added-bonus. Every year a dance would take place in the tent on the Saturday night; most of the adults from the parish would be there, and in the morning's early hours, once the music finished, they'd walk unsteadily back to their vehicles. We'd take advantage of the fact that most of them were half cut and charge them a fee to leave. Some would tell us to go away in no uncertain tone, but others would search around in their pockets for any notes or change they had, it was a good money-making scheme, and we'd been known to take home four times as much as the weekend's organisers were prepared to pay us for our nights work.

Rabbit chirped in "I've got a great idea" he said. "I know where they store all the excess wine for the dance. It's all kept in the village hall. I heard a couple of the old women from the PTA chatting about it at the Alligator last night. It's all delivered on Friday afternoon. It's all kept up there. They only go to fetch it once the bar has run dry in the marquee. The dance starts at eight, we can make sure all the cars are parked up by then, and then get ourselves up to the village hall and nick the vino. It won't be until around eleven when they'll need to restock and that is plenty of time to get in and out with the lot." "But how do we get in there?" Seth asked. "My mum is one of the people with keys to the hall" I said, "I can get hold of her set no problem".

And so, it was decided, the five of us were going to rob the village of a huge amount of alcohol – what we did with it once we'd got it, I didn't know but it sounded like a good plan to us. We weren't exactly well behaved, but we weren't criminals either, we'd never robbed anywhere before – This was scary stuff, and I'm pretty sure we were all terrified. I know I was, but male bravado took over and neither of us want to look weak in front of the others. Pat was convinced we could sell the stuff we hadn't drank and make some money, but the local youth club attendees didn't earn a wage. This would take some serious thinking but for now the plan was in place to steal the alcohol and enjoy the bounty as much as we could.

Over the next couple of days, we enjoyed everything the village had to offer. Ever since we were young kids, we'd welcomed this festival as the event of the summer. In our minds and for this short period of time, our parish was the centre of the universe, and we intended to make the most of it. The school days dragged as I looked forward to the evenings and the merriment over on the playing fields.

Thursday June 11th

On the afternoon of Thursday June 11th, the marquee was open to all. The local historical society had put on an event alongside the yearly art exhibition. There were postcards and photos from the village's past, which included pictures of relatives of many of the locals. Things like this were usually only of great interest to the older generation but I also had an interest in local history this year, because I was putting together a project for school that looked back at the Danehill of yesteryear. I attended after school to help my mum serve drinks, cakes, and the like to the attendees, before strolling around the exhibits to take in some culture. I started chatting with the chairman of the historical society to get some inside knowledge for my assignment. There was one hundred years of history on display. I asked why there was only a century of information to view and was told that this was as far back as they could find in the archives. He said that they had done a lot of research to find out information prior to 1887 but there was nothing. They had been to Kew in West London and scrutinised the national archives and observed nothing that indicated our village existed before October 1887, hence the reason why this year was Danehill's 100th birthday. I did an interview with the chairman and returned home with a few brochures and photos contented that I had enough to start researching my school project.

Thursday evening was nothing special for the local youths; an auction of promises, that raised money for communal groups and charities. The whole atmosphere and the fact that everybody attended however made up for that. We all went and spent most of the night persuading our dads to buy us beers from the bar. Carter's old man soon gave in, just to keep us quiet, and Seth ended up bidding (And winning) for a meal for two at the local pub. We all left before the end, as Seth knew he didn't have the means to pay for it. From what we heard Carter's dad ended up paying for that too!

Friday June 12th

The Friday night was different though. This was our evening this was the disco to end all discos. Youngsters came from all the surrounding places to attend – You must understand; this was Sussex in 1987 – There was not exactly much to do for kids of our age. One bus an hour into the local town – the last one left at 5pm. A cycle into town; this took an hour. The nearest train station - 10 miles away. We were home birds by circumstance, so the disco meant fun on our own turf with visitors from far and wide – and this meant females, and lots of them.

I got home from school and began my plan for the evening, which had been prepared meticulously. Homework – ignore, tea at 5.30, bath at 6. Next up, black flecked trousers on and retrieve green short sleeved shirt from the hanger, which mum had already ironed and pressed. There was no way I'd fail to attract the girls tonight, especially after the Insignia after shave had been applied. We all met up outside the tent at 7pm. There was a lot of hanging about on the recreation ground – nobody wanted to enter the marquee first to be labelled a square. Cider was being drunk; fags were being smoked and lads were showing off – it was a typical beginning to a teenage evening. The five of us casually strolled across the playing field, checking over the out-of-town visitors. Pat had raided his parent's drinks cabinet and made a concoction of spirits that shouldn't have been drank by anybody in their right mind, this was mixed with orange squash to temper the taste of the extremely odd blend of rum, vodka, whisky and malibu. But as every English teenager knew this was the best and cheapest way of consuming alcohol.

There were girls galore and we didn't miss a beat. We thought we were invincible, and every single one got a wink and a hello from us as they made their way into the canvassed venue. At around 8pm, and with all the alcohol drunk we made our way onto the dancefloor as 'Pump up the Jam' pulsated from the speakers. It was a great night; we knew the DJ, a local fella, from down our street – he was giving us shout outs. We felt like Kings. It was as though everybody knew who we were. People from the village would come up and say hi, the girls would dance nearby gyrating against us all – I felt like a 15- year-old version of Patrick Swayze. We went through the whole repertoire from Star Trekking to La Isla Bonita by Madonna, and La Bamba, plus the Mel and Kim classic Respectable – the Ashdown weekend of 1987 felt like the beginning of our lives. But beyond all this bluster there was always the lingering anticipation of our very own planned heist that was to come on the Saturday night.

At 11pm, the music was still going strong but some of us had retired outside - Pat was still on the dance floor smooching some girl from a nearby village. Somebody had lit a fire in the corner of the playing fields, and we sat around keeping warm. Seth, Carter, Rabbit, and I had failed to meet anyone of the female persuasion, but we'd had a night like no other "The best party ever" Seth noted. We all agreed but the excitement and trepidation of the following evening was on all our minds. Carter was first to break,

"How's everybody feeling about tomorrow night"?" I'm feeling confident" I said, "I've found out where mum keeps the keys, this time tomorrow we are going to have so much booze. We can sell a load and make a fortune, and we are going to have such a party tomorrow night". Rabbit interrupted me, "We should put up a tent of our own and camp for the night". Seth said that he thought he knew somebody who would buy all the stolen alcohol from us. "I've spoken to Toggy, he said he'd give us a good price." Toggy owned another local pub, 'The Wagon and Ponies' and was a bit of a dodgy character – none of us doubted Seth when he mentioned his moniker.

There was another, much larger, group of youngsters, around a much larger fire just to our right. We vaguely knew a few of them, they were locals but very different to us – they all lived in the big houses with the swimming pools and big dogs and attended a nearby private school by the name of Cobnor House. One of them was Giles Smedley, he looked over and gave us all a thumbs up, we responded in kind. Giles was sipping from a wine bottle. "Why does he always drink wine?" I said "Does he think he's got more class than us? I've never seen him swigging from a beer can." They weren't mates of ours, but we knew who they were, they were harmless. "Do you think he heard what we were talking about?" Rabbit said. "I can't hear myself think, let alone listen to any of your old rubbish" I replied. If Giles had heard us, he hadn't let on. "We should sell them the booze" Seth said. "We could make double what Toggy would pay, they might go to Cobnor, but they've got no common sense, not a brain cell between them". We all laughed.

It was approaching 11.30 so we all went back into the tent to see if there was any chance of a late snog when the slow dance tracks came on but by the time we entered the tent we saw that the disco had ended abruptly. Pat had got into a disagreement with a lad from Worsted Haynes, a neighbouring village, a fight had ensued. Pat decided to take matters into his own hands and literally pulled the plug on the party, he'd found the electricity cupboard and smashed and destroyed the whole thing – There would be no more dancing tonight, so we all strolled home. It was typical Pat; if he wasn't going to be having fun, then nobody else was either! We walked over to the playing fields exit and said our goodbyes before jumping the gate and heading home. We were all nervous, but nobody wanted to admit it. We all knew that what we had planned was nothing compared to the odd fight or the occasional night of under-age drinking – This was serious stuff, and the repercussions would be serious if we were caught.

Saturday June 13th

I woke up quite early on the Saturday. I had a sore head, but mum had a fry up ready when I got downstairs. Within an hour I was ready to face the day. We obviously had a big night planned but before that we had the annual Ashdown weekend 5-a-side football competition to win.

I met the boys on the playing field at 11. It was a bright sunny day, and the turnout was much as expected, one to two hundred people filled the area around the tent registering tournament entries. There was something quite comforting about this – everybody there, the sun shining, people excited about the afternoon ahead. This yearly event had always appealed to me, but the football, in particular. I'd always loved the game and knowing that the whole village would be watching thrilled me. It was like our own World Cup. Teams from all over the area would enter their 5 names and look to fight for glory. It was a safety net, and I felt secure. All the locals would be right behind the teams from our village and cheer us on. I hoped that one day I'd leave and go onto bigger and better things, the fluffy comfort blanket of the village had held me close but as I got older, I'd began to realise that I was destined for better things.

You would have thought that I'd be having regrets about what we had planned to do that night, but the thrill of the evening ahead had got the better of me. I felt older somehow, I felt like this was the beginning, and that I was ready to start my life as a different, more mature person, albeit as a bit of a minor criminal.

The football was as good as ever; we eased our way through the early rounds and came up against a side from Worsted Haynes in the semi-final, it was a battle of attrition. Matches against our local rivals were always tense and usually ended with a punch-up. The intensity of this 5-a-side game magnified in the searing heat of a June afternoon and with tempers frayed, the inevitable occurred. One red card for each team, a missed penalty for them and a scored penalty for us meant we won through to the final.

There were 2 sides to our street – We were known as Buckingham Palace Road by the other side of the street, this was because our parents had the foresight to begin to buy their properties from the council – this apparently made us posh and rich. The actual name of our road was Oak Tree Cottages, but that didn't matter to them.

Of course we ended up playing these neighbours in the final. We lost, and the opposition made the most of it, taunting us throughout. It wasn't much fun – kicks were aimed, punches were thrown, and spectators got involved in the scuffles – It wasn't the best way to end the competition, and somehow, we'd have to find a way to repay them for their over-zealous and rough house footballing tactics.

We finished the football and walked across the recreation ground about 4pm – it was still warm, and people were enjoying the fete, which had been running alongside the tournament that afternoon. There was joy in the air, the bar area was rammed with villagers enjoying themselves - some a little too much. Music was playing and sausages and hamburgers were being grilled on the huge barbecue. That comfy blanket of village life was in full swing – everybody knew everybody else, and your business didn't belong only to you for too long. Tonight, however, we were breaking free, and not a soul had even an inkling of what we were planning. Our little adventure was to shake our tiny village to its very core, but for now it was just us five lads with the knowledge of the night ahead and our mischievous plan.

Inside the marquee arrangements were being made for the adults highlight of the weekend – the dance – a chance for the parents to don black tie and sequined gowns. They would let their hair down for the evening. No kids were allowed to enter the tent on the Saturday night, this was their event. Tables were being decorated and the tent poles were adorned with sashes and giant bows. The bar was being stacked with alcohol, and the band were setting up their equipment on the stage, no doubt revelry would ensue. As I walked past the entrance to the tent my dad called out to me; he was inside the tent, lending a hand "Sam, can you nip home please? Your mum has driven your sister to the video shop, and I've forgotten my toolbox. It's in the garage". This was manna from Heaven for me, an opportunity to get the keys to the village hall, it was too good to be true. I gave the boys a wink and ran the short distance home. Once inside I went straight to the giant wooden key, we had above the coal cupboard in the kitchen. This is where all the keys were kept hanging – this was too easy – I grabbed the keys to the village hall and went out to the garage to fetch dad's toolbox – As I grabbed hold of the heavy garage door to manoeuvre it up and over, I sensed I was being watched. I turned around but couldn't see anything untoward. So, I took the box from its position on the shelf and made my way out onto the drive, turning back to quickly grab a torch as I thought that might come in handy later. Before I returned to the playing field, I safely hid the key and the torch behind the village bus shelter and made my way back to see dad. The heist was now in motion.

Later that night Seth, Carter, Rabbit, Pat, and I were in our usual place on the rec, seeing cars into the car park, and making sure they manoeuvred their vehicles into the correct spots. We knew a lot of the locals, and what they would be doing later. For instance, some were accustomed to a heavy night of drinking, and they would be instructed park right at the back, as there was no way they would be driving home later. Others who we were maybe not so keen on would be advised to park in spots that we knew would be very difficult to get out of later. There was a camaraderie between all the kids on patrol, and we spent most of the evening in absolute hysterics.

Once the party goers were all safely inside the tent, we could really start to enjoy ourselves. Pat had managed to goad a few car owners to leave their keys safely in his grasp to ensure that they weren't tempted to drive back to their homestead in the early hours of the morning. He took great delight in showing us his prowess and masterfulness of hand brake turns around the playing field. Everybody had raided drinks cabinets at home and much alcohol was drunk. The atmosphere was brilliant, as usual, and the music from the marquee reverberated around the village and the laughter and chatter from the tent indicated that the dance was in full swing. At 10 o'clock most of the car park stewards had now returned to their houses, and there were only a few of us left on site. The five of us pitched our tent on the edge of the woods ready for later and prepared ourselves for the biggest night of our lives.

We had roughly forty-five minutes until the barmen would make their way up to the village hall to replenish their supplies. The memorial hall as it was also known, was built in the 1920's. If there was ever a birthday celebration or a Christmas party, it was always hosted there. We had put on school plays on the stage, we had danced at weddings and discos there. We had been to christening parties and even wakes in the hall. It really was the central point of the village and the whole community. We knew it like the back of our hands, and now we were going to rob it. It felt bad, almost as though we were cheating on ourselves. But we didn't weren't thinking about sentimentality now, we just wanted the alcohol and the cash.

It was just a ten-minute dash walk from the recreation ground to the hall, and once inside, it wouldn't take us long to empty the storage space where we thought the alcohol was stockpiled. It was dark but the light from the ongoing shindig in the marquee ensured the route was well lit – we were familiar with the stroll up the hill having all lived in Danehill since birth, but the brightness from the tent made it an even easier navigation, and we were soon face to face with the doors of the village hall and the stash inside that we hoped would make us an abundance of money. It wouldn't be a fortune, but we all imagined the summer of parties, holidays, and fun we would have once we'd sold the proceeds of our deft robbery.

I left the boys outside the hall and slid down the bank to the side of the car park to retrieve the key and the torch from their hiding place behind the bus stop. I heard a noise as I made my way down the slippery bank but was relieved to see it was just a badger – he stared angrily at me for disturbing his sleep, there was a stand-off for a moment, but he soon got bored, and on I went. The bank was sheltered by brambles and branches, which didn't make this an easy access point to the bus shelter, but if I'd have taken the route along the road I'd have been spotted by the drinkers outside the Alligator; where there were a small number of locals who obviously had no desire to attend the dance. I dodged my way around a huge pile of white dog dirt, that seemed to glow in the dark, and I heard a rip of paper as I almost lost my footing whilst slipping on a left-over pornographic magazine.

I eventually got down to the bottom of the bank and grabbed the tools I'd hidden and scrambled my way back up to meet the others and was ridiculed for the mud and branches that had affixed itself to my hair. I pushed the key in the lock and turned it, but it wouldn't budge. I tried again, and to my horror – nothing. Rabbit was agitated "Try it again!" I did but still nothing – The key was stuck. Carter grabbed at the large iron door handles and pulled, hoping to dislodge the key. "I reckon you've picked up the wrong key Sam" Rabbit said. We were starting to panic now, I seized hold of the key and tried to turn it the other way, it snapped off in my hand, I froze, shocked at what had just happened. We had failed at the first hurdle. Even though I was facing away, I could sense the boy's eyes angrily staring right through the back of me, this was my fault, and I had let them all down. There wasn't enough time to return home to find the actual set of keys, we had about half an hour before the barmen came to collect the spare drink. then a sudden loud smash stopped us in our tracks.

Seth had thrown a brick through the window. "Come on lads" he cried, "In we go". He pulled down his sleeve and hastily moved aside the shattered glass and jumped up to allow himself enough room to open reach inside and open the window clasp, and clamber in. Once into the hall he came around to the main doors and let us all in. "Thanks mate" I said. "No problem" Seth replied, "But let's do this quick, before the boozers come and have a look at what we're up to. That smash must have made a right racker".

Once inside I scampered over to one of the large windows that faced the pub; luckily the only person left outside the pub was the local alcoholic Mickey Hamble, and he was falling asleep on the bench. There was no way he would have heard a thing. We all stepped into the vast emptiness of the village hall. It seemed larger than usual, we were used to seeing this room full of villagers at local pantomimes, exhibitions or plays. It seemed strangely quiet on this Saturday night. Though we could all hear the faint sound of music from the marquee, the unoccupied room gave the impression of an eery atmosphere. Maybe it was the fact that we knew we were doing something that was alien to us, and incredibly risky, but there was something else that gave out an air of abnormality. We all felt it but none of us said a word, we stared at each other for a few moments and then our brains clicked into gear – operation alcohol was what we came for and operation alcohol is what we needed to do.

In the corner of the hall was a wooden plinth, and on top of that was an old, slightly deflated football and four crates of lager and bitter. If this was all that was stored here then this whole escapade had been a total waste of time, and an utter disaster. We frantically searched the rest of the hall. We looked around the men's and lady's toilets, we searched the kitchen, and we looked in the stock room but could find nothing. It seemed that all the alcohol had already left here and had been in the tent the whole evening. This meant two things – that we wouldn't get caught in the act, so there was no need to hurry - but also that we weren't going to make a windfall from selling our wares. We were gutted, but it had still been fun, so there was only one thing for it, we cracked open the cans and began to have a little party of our own. As more and more of the beer was drunk, we started to forget the disappointment and enjoy the time we were having. It still felt quite daring; breaking into a municipal building and consuming drink that didn't belong to us.

A game of football soon transpired, and as happens when boys will be boys it started to get quite ferocious. Not in a nasty way, just in the way that mates are with each other. It was all good humoured and fun, but it seemed obvious that a window could easily be smashed, or a fire extinguisher might be set off as our game became more and more passionate. Carter was strolling cooly around, beer can in hand showing off his skills with the ball and was almost robbed by the chunky legs of Seth. Pat was not exactly known for his sporting prowess, and he was next in line to stop Carter, the rest of us took great pleasure on seeing him tackle his friend so easily. He launched himself forward and took one hell of a swipe at the football. It flew at break-neck speed, and pile drove into the stage smashing one of the panels wide open. The panel splintered and the large wooden jagged shards exposed the darkness behind the front of the stage of Danehill Village Hall.

We all laughed at the absurdity of the situation. Pat's surprising initial footballing prowess had once away given way to his usual ineptitude with a ball, and he had broken the stage in the process. The game soon continued until Rabbit beckoned us over to inspect the newly manmade hole. "Can you feel the force of that wind? It's icy cold, and strong". He was right. Next, he shouted "HELLO". Hello, hello, hello echoed back at him. "Why is there such an echo"? Seth responded. We all weighed in and started frantically pulling on all the panels exposing the emptiness behind. Carter grabbed the torch, and we all sidled closer to the edge on our stomach's and lent over to see what state the ground might be in beneath the old stage. Carter shone the torch down, and it caught something glistening below. The hole below us was huge and as we lent further in to see what the torch had revealed, the earth started to cave in. We were lucky not to fall and would have done if we'd have been standing.

And that was when our eyes caught sight of it for the very first time. Where once the dais had stood firm whilst local dramatists acted out everything from Old Mother Hubbard and Joseph and the amazing technicolour dream coat to a very modern and peculiar version of Cats the musical, below it was now what seemed to be the resting place of far more jewellery and antiques than you would find in Claridges. Our plans to steal and sell beer has been thwarted but somehow, we had stumbled upon enough bounty to secure our lives forever. A whole treasure trove of wonderment was laid out down below us. The hole must have been 50 feet deep. We couldn't quite see the whole hoard, but once Seth had switched on the main hall lights, we were able to take most of it. It was like something you'd see in a fairy story – There were piles upon piles of gold coins. There were antique vases, there was jewellery and old-fashioned furniture, it was outrageous but beautiful.

Our eyes were now accustomed to the light, and we had much more of an idea of our surroundings. We peered down below us, each staring at one and other. Carter was the first to let go – he let out a huge scream of delight, and we all followed. It was astounding. We hugged each other and continued to shout and yell. Pat stared down below in disbelief "Well boys, I suppose we're millionaires then". We all laughed. This was the most exciting thing to have happened to us in a long, long time.

But we still had some decisions to make. How would we get all of this out? How would we keep this quiet? How would we make money from this? But above all, there was excitement – After all, we had found it. No matter what anybody else in the village said, surely this was ours now. And then we saw it. "Obviously somebody else knows all this lot this is here," said Carter. "Look down, there's a ladder attached to the wall. And there's fag ends, modern wine bottles and an old broadsheet newspaper." He was correct but why did that matter? "So what?" I replied. "Finders, keepers and all that". "We can't just take it all," said Carter. "We'll get spotted, it will take us months to move all of this. What are we gonna use? Wheelbarrows? Cardboard boxes? We need a plan".

Monday June 22nd

It had been over a week now, a week since we'd come across the treasures and exposed the deep hole beneath the village hall. The plan was to cover the hole in the stage back up and not tell a soul what had occurred. Seth and Carter got hold of some wood from a local timber yard and made a makeshift cover for the gap. We'd keep a keen eye on the building for a few days and made sure that nobody went inside. We wanted to unearth out who knew about the find before us but were more concerned that they'd go in and discover that we'd discovered it. The village hall wasn't in use that regularly so we felt safe in the knowledge that all would be okay. The only issue we could see was moving the trove before anyone noticed what we'd exposed. Rabbit had taken a closer look at the discarded rubbish in the hole and the newspaper he'd eyed was dated April 1986, so we were confident that whoever knew of this ahead of us wasn't a regular visitor to the site. Next, we had to figure out how we would move everything, and how we would do it without being found out. There was also the problem of where we would put it all.

Thursday June 25th

Three days later we had an arrangement in place to transport and store the goods. We let a local friend in on the secret. Ronny Braker could be trusted, he was someone we'd all known for years and was an aspiring carpenter. It was crucial that we didn't get any adults involved in our cloak-and-dagger operation, and Ronny was the perfect partner. His carpentry skills may come in handy later too. His younger brother was a fan all things farming, and Ronny's dad had bought him a tractor and trailer. Pat's family owned a dog kennels and business wasn't good. A lot of the kennels were empty. This was Thatcher's Britain, and we were in the middle of a recession, families were not going on holiday, and many of the kennels were empty. So, now we had wheels and a spot to hide the loot. We could store the treasure at the kennels until we had formulated a plan of what we would do with it. We decided to launch the covert operation under the cover of darkness, and on that rainy Thursday night we all met up at the village hall ready to begin the latest stage of our plan.

It was lucky for us that the weather was dreadful. As I mentioned before, Danehill was a village that was full of people with little to do with their time. If something out of the ordinary was happening, then the whole place would know about it within hours. The noise of the downpour made it much easier for us to keep the whole process under wraps. Ronny had waited for his family to go to bed before jumping aboard his brother's vehicle. It was raining but he'd kept it safe by carefully releasing the hand brake and reversing down the steep drive of his home. It wasn't until he had reached the main road that he started up the engine of the 1972 John Deer tractor. The motor slowly chugged itself to life and Ronny drove the one and a half miles up the hill to the village hall, his parents would be none the wiser.

We were all waiting in the car park, thankful for the rain and thankful for the umbrella's that Rabbit had bought along from home. We were dry and keen to get this completed before the weather improved, and the rain stopped. It was eleven thirty and we waited patiently for the last light to turn out inside the upstairs living accommodation of the Alligator. We then had to wait an extra thirty minutes to give the landlord time to get to bed and fall asleep. The rain was still pelting down onto the tarmac of the car park, and making a racket, but we wanted to ensure that this all went perfectly. The rain acted as a good shelter for the noise, and we knew that just the slightest bit of noise could endanger the whole plot. Once inside, we dismantled the stage. Ronny was as astonished as we were initially to what could be seen beneath the stage. We'd promised him a small part of the treasure as payment for helping us and he seemed happy with that, although once he'd seen what was on offer, I'm pretty sure he wished he'd haggled us for more.

Friday June 26th

By now it had gone midnight, and there was still a lot to do. Seth climbed down the ladder and into the depths of the hole below. We each shimmied our way down to make a chain gang with each of us separated by a few rungs on the ladder. We then passed on the items up the line one by one to Ronny, who was atop the ladder inside the village hall.

Initially we sent up the smaller items such as jewellery, clothing, books, papers, and objects d'art. These were obviously much easier to move. The many paintings came next, we weren't exactly experts but from reading the signatures on some of the paintings we could tell that these would be worth some money. There were landscapes by Turner and Constable, which if the real deal, would fetch a pretty penny at auction. There were medals from various wars too. This was a very interesting haul, there were diaries dating back hundreds of years, which we would put aside to investigate later. The last of the plenteousness was already in large metal boxes, which was handy but also heavy. These were right at the bottom of the hole, so we decided to tow these out. We opened the huge double doors of the village hall and Ronny backed the tractor up nearer to the exit. We used the rope in the back of the trailer to tie the containers and haul them out. Seth was keen to see what was inside of these large boxes and took an axe to the metal locks that were keeping them secure. They broke open easily, and out fell thousands and thousands of old coins, with some dating back as far as 1850. Others were so old that they didn't even have a date on them. There were 6 storage boxes of these coins – we had literally struck gold.

Saturday June 27th

By four o'clock in the morning there was a huge accumulation of riches inside the room above, ready to be escorted away in the tractor. We were all exhausted, but our comfy beds and sleep would have to wait. The downpour had now stopped, and we estimated that it would take seven or eight journeys back and forth to the kennels, and we'd be done by the time the sun had risen and welcomed a new summer day into our homes.

Ronny started up the tractor, whilst Carter locked up the village hall, and we all leapt up onto the trailer to begin the first delivery of goods to Pat's family home. His parent's had made the most of the business being quiet and taken a break to spend some time with Pat's grandparents at the other side of the county. The only person at that end of the deliveries was Chole, she was the girl hired to look after the kennels and had a soft spot for Pat. We arrived at the kennels ten minutes later and dropped off the first cargo. Pat and Seth stayed behind to put the goods into the empty kennels and the rest of us headed back to the centre of the village to fetch the next load. It took longer this time, but we stored the trailer with another batch of containers and headed back. By the time we reached the kennels on Fanyard Lane Seth was alone. We asked where Pat was, and he explained that Chloe had woken up and ventured outside to see what all the fuss was about. "Pat decided to use his charm." Seth commented. "He's now inside with Chole, it was the only way of keeping her quiet". We all laughed. We were a man down, so things were going to take longer still but we were well on our way.

By six am we had moved all but one of the loads of treasure from the village hall to the kennels. We carefully stored the last of the boxes of coins onto the back of the tractor and jumped on, Ronny drove us about 200 yards down the road and we heard a spluttering. The tractor stopped. He turned the key nothing happened. He looked at the gauge, the petrol tank was empty. The sun was up soon, and we were concerned. The village would be coming to life soon and we hadn't finished. Rabbit panicked, "What are we going to do?" I don't know why or how I thought of it at this time in the morning with no sleep, but I had the answer,

"We need to syphon some petrol from another tank" I said. "You get an empty can and something like a straw and suck on the straw, until you taste the petrol, then quickly put the straw into the empty can." We needed a receptacle, and a car full of petrol!"

We had stopped in the middle of the main road; this was not good. We had a trailer piled up with God knows what and people were going to be asking questions if we were spotted. Carter jumped out the back and started trying to push the vehicle, he was desperate. "That's never gonna work", Ronny was feeling uneasy now. "That's the vicarage" he said after a short while. "Come on lads, let's empty David Kendall's petrol tank. If anybody is going to forgive us, it's the vicar!". Ronny's brother had an old ice cream tub full of random nails and screws etc. "Use this" Ronny said, as he tipped the objects into the trailer. So, off I went, ice cream tub in hand, I felt awful, but I needed to do this. The others had a close shave as I wandered away to the vicarage when the local paperboy cycled passed. Barry Dawson paused briefly, looked at the situation before him, and then rode off. Quite what he thought, we never knew, but luckily for us he didn't take any notice of the big tractor crammed to the hilt with treasure, sitting in the middle of the road with three people he knew standing, and looking agitated nearby. He cycled off at speed at breakneck speed with a wave and a "goodbye", on his way to deliver the morning newspapers. By the time I returned to the boys we could hear the cockerel's singing their morning song. I made it back into the tractor cab just in time, and once again we started our final journey back to the kennels. As we drove around the bend and past the cemetery, we could hear alarm clocks and could make out the shadows of people through their net curtains getting ready to start their day. As we approached the top of Fanyard Lane we were overtaken by two delivery vehicles. We had made it out by the skin of our teeth.

Sunday June 28th

We unloaded the rest of the consignment into the empty kennels, and all returned home to our beds to try at least get some semblance of sleep. I couldn't rest though, I was excited. I wanted to get back to Pat's as soon as possible and begin to make plans on what we could do with all this treasure. There was also a nagging feeling at the back of my brain, a nagging feeling that was telling me somebody or more likely more than a few people also knew of this hoard. And they wouldn't be happy once they knew that it had gone. It could be a hiding place for burglar's loot, it could be a place where somebody was hiding their riches for a particular reason, it might also have belonged to the parish council. Whichever it was, it was obvious to me that somebody, at some point was going to come looking for it. And when they did, we had to be ready.

We had arranged to meet back at the kennels later that afternoon, but I couldn't wait and was back at Pat's place by two o'clock. It was no surprise that everybody was there when I arrived. We had all been far too enthusiastic about what we had found, and we all wanted to get together as soon as possible. Seth and Carter hadn't even made it home before turning round and headed back to Fanyard Lane within minutes of leaving. They had started sorting the goods into separate kennels depending on what was what. Pat had paid Chloe off. She had realised we were up to something but didn't know quite what. Luckily for us she wasn't one to pry. Pat told her that as things were quiet, and his parents were away that he could take care of things at the kennels for a few days. She pocketed thirty pounds from the petty cash and was soon on her way.

We spent the afternoon sorting through the stuff we'd plundered from the village hall. There was a feeling of exhilaration in the air. We had come across a dream find, a find that could easily change the lives of us and our families forever. It was like a party outside the kennels, we had much work to do but we did it with smiles on our faces. Many beers were drunk, and songs sang as we happily went about arranging the various troves into the kennels. Carter and I were trying to work out a way of categorising all the jewellery – There was so much of it – all from different eras, and all made from different metals. There was ruby's, there was solid gold and silver rings and bracelets and broaches, there were diamond earrings and watches – pocket watches, wrist watches, a carriage clock, a grandfather clock. Hilariously Pat was trying on the women's clothing – it all looked old, and moth ridden but you never know – these garments could be worth as much as the St. George's cross medal that Seth had pinned to his camouflage jacket. Rabbit took great joy in counting out the coins and old notes. He'd bought a book from home, which told him the worth of old monies. Every so often he'd yet out a yell. "Another two grand for that one lad's" There was much hilarity, and it soon became clear that there was much more here than we had originally thought. It was going to take a good few days before this was all in order, so we set about categorising the finds, and sorting out what we could sell, and how much we reckoned we could make.

Thursday July 2nd

Rabbit was currently learning to drive and had 'borrowed' his mums Volkswagen Beetle. He attached the learner plates, and the as he turned the keys it spluttered into life. It took three times to start the old 1965 engine, and we were soon off to the coast. It was a tight fit with three of us in the back of this vintage classic car. We'd been in touch with a dealer down in Brighton. He'd said he'd look at some of our items. We'd filled the smallish boot of the vehicle and loaded bags of swag around our heads and down by our feet. The beetle was ram packed with goods. There were old war medals, antique candle snuffers, old chinaware, mini statuettes, and a few small paintings in their original frames.

Rabbit squeezed the car into a very tight spot just off the Lewes Road in Brighton. It was a really hot day, and as we made our way down to the sea front, laden with bags and boxes we were greeted with the familiar sounds, scenes, and smells of Brighton; the skateboarders on 'The Level' daring to wheel their way down the massive half pipe. The infamous Grubs burger joint, and the smell of the fried onions wafting through the air, the dirty looking tattoo parlour and the two betting shops, the local looneys with their shopping trolleys full of Coca Cola cans and newspapers. The sound of the seagulls so prominent, the town of Brighton was alive with tourists and locals. It all felt so recognizable but somehow, also very different. Something had changed in me. I felt confident, and I walked tall. I looked across at the other four boys as we marched assertively down to the ocean. I smiled to myself. I could tell that they felt the same. We were going places, there was an air or reverence about us. We were feeling good, and nobody was getting in our way. It was unnerving but also brilliant.

The shop was easy to find. There was a tiny door by the side of a fish and chip shop just off the Old Steine on Prince's Street. Inside was like an Aladdin's cave. From the outside you'd think this was a very small dwelling, but once inside it seemed to stretch on forever. The walls were full of hooks with many old relics hanging down which made it look like a corridor of tree branches in a jungle. The lights were dim, which made the whole place even more mysterious, with only the odd retro neon sign lighting up tiny parts of the room. The floor was packed with even more old artifacts. We instigated our way through, past the antique elephant's footrest and the mannequin dressed as a woman from Moulin Rouge until we reached the very end of this long thin tunnelling like room. There was a shabby desk, and behind it sat an old man. He was short and plump, and wore glasses, which rested on the arch of his stumped nose, his green eyes peering out over the top of them.

His name was Eddie, and he was well-known in Brighton. He was the man you went to when you wanted information on the South Coast. We didn't know him personally, but we had heard his name many times over the years. Carter's dad Connor knew Eddie, and that is how we got hold of him. Connor wouldn't miss his address book. We had only borrowed it for a couple of days after all. Eddie was a unique character who was trusted by both the local constabulary, and the Sussex criminal underworld. We weren't sure whether we'd be safe in his presence but the fact that Connor was a friend of his meant that, hopefully, he'd treat us fairly. "Which one of you is Connor's boy then?" he said in a proper Sussex accent.

Eddie was surprised at our massive hoard. You could sense the excitement in his voice when he agreed to set about valuing the goods we'd presented him with. He suggested we made ourselves comfortable in the café opposite; this was going to take him a while. We all left him to it and visited the small cafe across the road to take stock. We sat at one of the tables outside the coffee shop watching the World go by. There was just one thing on our minds, as there always was – Our massive find. We were happy that Eddie was now involved but we needed to find other ways to value the rest of the gear. As we sat and pondered it was decided that we would take the larger paintings to auction, and get the coins valued by an expert. Some of the smaller stuff could be sold via local newspapers and we'd reach out to Eddie for ideas on what to do with the rest. We left the street and decided to take a stroll along the beach. We walked along the promenade and bought ice creams before skimming some pebbles out across the sea. Brighton always felt so alive, especially for five lads who had grown up in the countryside. We knew the town well and always enjoyed it's company. This time it seemed different. We had grown up over the past fortnight, and I felt that we were now giving off a different impression of ourselves. We were only a couple of weeks older but this whole scenario had changed us. We were braver now and felt more ready for what life had to throw at us. Whatever happened, we were sure we'd cope. The Danehill boys were up for the challenge, up for the fight and were excited for more.

By mid-afternoon we were back in Eddies office. He looked self-assured as he sat cross legged behind his desk. A month ago, we'd have been standing here nervously looking around, questioning why we were there. Today, we were in total control. "So, what do you reckon then Eddie?" said Rabbit. "How much do you reckon we'll get for it all?". Eddie was taken aback, he wasn't used to people being so blasé around him, but I believe he respected us at this moment. Five lads dressed in shorts and trainers, we didn't look the part but boy, we were playing it. "I have had a thorough look at the lot. You have got some good material here" he said. He explained that a lot of the stuff was very old and very rare and would fetch a pretty penny. He knew where to sell it whereas we didn't. We would lose some capital if we sold to Eddie, but he was a man that could – we were lads that couldn't. "I'll give you £30,000 for the lot" Eddie said.

It wasn't until we got back to the Beetle that we let ourselves go. "I can't believe it" Carter said "£32,000 smackers – yes!" We all screamed and shouted we were jubilant. "How on earth did we manage to hold our nerve in there?" Seth was laughing. "I almost fainted". Rabbit was proud of himself "I'm still trembling, I can't believe I asked for 35K". "I know" I said, "I thought he'd throw us out on the spot but fair play mate, that was brilliant". The journey home was the best drive I have ever had. We were all in great spirits. We cruised (as much as you can cruise in an old VW Beetle) over the South Downs with the windows down, and the music up. We were happy, the plan was going well. And now we had £32,000 to spend. This was huge money in 1987, especially to five teenage boys with many dreams. We stopped on the top of Devils Dyke for a pint and raised our glasses to us - This was going to be a good weekend.

Thursday July 9th

Four of us were now back at school. The summer holidays would be upon us very soon, so we'd have six weeks to enjoy our newly found fortune and make plans to sell the rest of our find. For now, though, we'd have to make do with going into school and keeping things as normal as possible. Pat managed to persuade his mum to give Rabbit a part time job at the kennels. He had already finished up his college for the year, so he was in sole charge of our new belongings. His part time job, from our point of view, would mainly involve keeping Pat's mum away from the supposedly empty kennels. It soon became clear that this wasn't going to work, and that we would need somewhere else for storage. Pat's mum was getting suspicious, and couldn't figure out why she wasn't getting anymore boarders booking in. Rabbit was fed up with running out to the phone every time it rang and lying to prospective customers about a full dog hotel. He felt rotten, especially in a recession. So, we decided to move all the gear. Rabbit then quit his new job. We put £500 in an envelope and left it for Pat's parents, we pretended it was from an anonymous tipper, with a note praising the work the family had done in looking after their canines. That made us feel much better about the whole situation.

During the second World War there was a training camp based in the village of Chelforest next to Danehill. It was used by Canadian soldiers and there was a huge outdoor swimming pool onsite. The place was called 'The Isle of Thorns' and was owned by a family from London with connections to the area. When the head of this family died in 1965, he had it written in his will that the local children should be able to use the facilities for free. So, from that day on and on every Monday and Thursday evening in the summer months, us kids were allowed to use the swimming pool. It was so much fun, and for many years this is what we did, twice a week. Sadly, in recent years, the swimming club had stopped, as people started to move on in the modern age. They wanted hot indoor pools with slides and log flumes so our twice weekly jaunt to the Isle of Thorns swimming baths came to an end. Luckily for us there was a massive area that consisted of a huge empty swimming pool and three changing rooms. It was clear of any humans and turned out to be the perfect spot. This was where we could now store our stolen stock.

So, that evening we loaded up Ronny's brother's tractor and drove from Fanyard Lane to the Isle of Thorns. It was 8 o'clock and we felt safe in the knowledge that we wouldn't look out of the ordinary at this time of night in the summer. In fact, we passed several tractors with loads of their own, going about their business. That was the benefit of living in the countryside with many farmers in the area, a tractor certainly didn't look out of place, not in the evening. We felt much more comfortable than we had when previously moving our shipment in the early hours of the morning. It took several loads before we were done, and we started out on the last shipment at around 11pm.

We left the kennels and made our way down towards the Wagon and Ponies pub. As we went around the bend we spotted a figure walking slowly along the road. It was clear it was a male, he was carrying a torch, and he was flashing the light at the tractor cab, motioning for us to come to a stop. As we approached, we realised it was Giles Smedley and he was carrying a rope and a toolbox. He was struggling and laden down. "Sorry guys, I thought you were somebody else" Giles said. "What are you doing out at this time with all that gear?" Ronny replied, "You look like you're going to rob a bank!". "I've got stuff to do" Giles explained, without explaining anything at all! "What are you lot up to?" "Same", Rabbit said. This seemed to suit both parties. We drove on down the hill. Thirty seconds later we were passed by another tractor. We watched it from the back of the trailer, and it came to a halt where Giles was now standing back up the road. "That was very odd" Carter mentioned. We all nodded in agreement. "It's not as if he's poor. Why would he be on the rob?" Carter sniggered. "Maybe he's a grave digger in his spare time."

Friday July 10th

It seemed like a good time to enjoy the fruits of our labour. So, this weekend was ours, we had £32,000 of hard cash and we planned to enjoy being rich. We had made a pact, a pact that that we needed to keep our fortune a secret for now. There was to be no spending big on stuff that would bring attention to the locals, of course we had dreams; dreams of buying flash cars, dreams of putting down a deposit on a shared flat for the 5 of us, dreams of holiday's abroad, but that was not wise at this juncture. We were still not sure why or how the treasure had ended up beneath the bowels of Danehill Village Hall, and we had no idea whatsoever who put it there. These people could be criminals, these people could be dangerous too. We hoped that they had long gone from history as the items we had taken were so old. We needed time to think but not yet, as we intended enjoying ourselves over this weekend as much as humanly possible.

We hit Brighton again on the Friday night. We were cash rich so booked a taxi to take us the twenty-five miles or so to the South Coast, making sure we booked an out-of-town firm to drive us. The film Predator was released that weekend, so we started off our evening by booking the best seats at the Odeon cinema to watch Arnold Schwarzenegger taking on an alien in the South American jungle. Next stop was Al Duomos, a traditional Italian restaurant by the Brighton pavilion. We ordered the biggest pizzas on the menu and all the trimmings – we felt like Kings. None of us were old enough to drink so we visited Eddie, who provided us all with fake identification. They looked so much better than Seth's current replica driving license. Eddie had become a very useful ally and would remain very helpful to us in the months to come. We certainly made the most that Brighton had to offer for the rest of the night. We went from pub to pub drinking all sorts of concoctions of cocktails and spirits, we danced our way around several clubs and chatted to girls galore. By the time we had finished it was 6am, and we made our way down to the beach and sat and watched the sun rise. It had been a glorious night. We sat in silence, and we all knew exactly what the others were thinking, we were happy and excited for what was to come. We could hear the faint noise of incessant acid house music pumping out from the clubs behind us. But we were too deep in thought to engage. By the time we left Brighton we had spent around £500 of our winnings, we had only just touched the surface of what we wanted to do, and what we sought to achieve. There were many more adventures to be had, and we were certainly going to have them. This voyage of discovery had only just begun.

Saturday July 11th

We all stayed the night at Seth's and started the following day off in his family swimming pool, cleansing ourselves of the excesses from the previous night's shenanigans. We were soon ready to get out and about again and spend more of the money. There wasn't a great deal to do around where we lived but we were used to this, so had much experience of making the most of our rather boring surroundings – the difference this time is that we had a bounty to squander on whatever we so desired. Seth wasn't old enough to drive but had an old Fiat 126 on his driveway. His parents were relaxed and let him drive the old banger if he didn't venture too far from home. We all clambered in the back and made our way to the local Little Chef café for a big breakfast whilst we planned the rest of our day of joyous spending. Pat grabbed a copy of the Friday Ad, one of the local papers from the newsstand. It was a paper where you could buy or sell almost anything to anyone. "I've got an idea, boys" he said with a big grin on his face.

We trawled the vehicles section of the newspaper. There were some very nice cars for sale, but they were not what we wanted. We had decided that a great way of having fun that afternoon was to buy some old automobiles and motor bikes so we could cause some carnage on the Ashdown Forest. There was an old air strip on the forest which had been used by the British army during the second World War. It wasn't far from the Isle of Thorns; I presume the landing strip was the place where the soldiers would come in on to do their training. We had often made our way up there when we had been much younger, we would ride our bikes up and down, our hair flowing in the breeze, it had always added much hilarity to our afternoons during the six-week long school summer holidays.

We came across a couple of old Mini's for sale in the nearby village of Putley. It would cost us just £400 for the pair, and Pat, Carter and Seth were soon driving over to Putley in the Fiat to pick them up. Meanwhile Rabbit, and I had made the short trip to Worsted Haynes to purchase a couple of clapped-out mopeds for £80. We spent much of the afternoon on the landing strip racing each other, stopping only to sup on cans of cheap lager from the local store. It might not seem extravagant, but to us, having the memory of cycling this spot as children, made it so much more, the fact that we could now afford to buy actual petrol fuelled vehicles was so invigorating. And the main fact was that we could have fun with our earnings without anyone knowing that we'd been spending vast amounts of our newly made monies.

Tuesday July 13th

Rabbit was having a nicely chilled summer and was enjoying having fun whilst we were all at school. It was also handy that he had plenty of spare time on his hands. He had completed his exams and had a long break ahead before starting further education at the local 6th form college. He was on hand to keep a keen eye on our treasure trove up at the old swimming baths. We had joked about buying him a security guard's uniform and a luminous Hi-Visual jacket. He'd sometimes get bored and surprise us all by turning up at our school, which was five or six miles away, and picking us up in his mum's Beetle. We'd drive home along the country roads playing music very loudly and blasting the cars horn at anyone who passed us. We would stop off in laybys and play football or cricket, and stuff our mouths with copious amounts of food. There was a local firm of pie makers called Lillies, and they created the best pies in the area. Rabbit would always ensure he'd stock the car with plenty of these before picking us up. We'd all return home to spend time with our families before heading out together until dark; It seemed like the evenings would never end. We'd all meet up and play football, drink lager, and generally do what all the other kids our age were doing. The difference was that we were rich, albeit secretly.

But over the next couple of weeks everything almost unravelled before our very eyes. We were bored and struggling to think of ideas of what we could get up to. We were all astutely aware that the weekend was nearly upon us, and that was when we changed. We changed from local kids in the village, to men about town. We all loved the weekends but, as we were having so much fun over those two days of the week, it meant that from Monday to Friday everything seemed so tame, and the weekdays dragged on. We were constantly aiming to do bigger and better things. We had all this dough, so we wanted to enjoy it to the fullest, but we also knew that we needed to keep everything quiet. Just one little sniff of something suspicious to a nosey villager could be disastrous for us and our future earnings, as well as our new joyous lives.

The garden at the Alligator was packed with locals enjoying the evening sunshine, and the five of us were sat at a table, each enjoying a glass of coke, topped-up with vodka from Carter's dad's drinks cabinet. It was around 6pm, and we were struggling with ideas in-order-to make the most of the night ahead. Tuesday nights were not exactly exciting in Danehill in 1987, and the thought of going home to watch Adrian Mole on the television was not exactly appealing. One of my neighbours Doreen Coates was keeping an eye on us, she could tell that we weren't just drinking pop. Doreen wasn't daft, and knew we were under-age, so we were trying to keep our alcohol sipping to a minimum – at least when she happened to look in our direction. Mickey Hamble was usually propping up the bar but even he had decided to venture outside to enjoy the warmth of the evening. He came and sat down at our table and began chatting away to us about nothing, whilst slurring his words. Hamble however did mention something that did pique an interest in us. He said that there was a local art dealer inside the pub, and that he was showing off about a painting he had sold at auction for a few thousand pounds. We made a mental note to find out who this guy was, as he could come in very handy in the future.

Mickey soon got agitated at the thought of not being near his beloved bar, and us not buying him a pint, and moved back inside to continue his nightly drinking spree. Doreen Coates did the decent thing and helped his stumbling body return to the saloon bar - we all took advantage of this and had an extra swig of vodka. Ronny Braker came sauntering over, he didn't look too well. "What's up Ronny"? I said "Bad news" Ronny replied "I don't think I'm going to be able to finish my carpentry course and get a job. They've added in an extra load of tools and materials to the syllabus and mum and dad can't afford to buy them, I'm stuffed".

Rabbit and I looked at each other and nodded. "We can sort that for you mate" Rabbit said "You have been an absolute star for us over the last few weeks. We'll help you. How much do you need?" "Really?" Ronny said. "That would be brilliant, thanks boys, I'll have to ring my tutor now. He's going to offer somebody my place tomorrow, so I'll have to let him know straightaway. It's £350. Are you sure?" "Go and call him now" Seth said. And off he went to the pay phone inside the pub.

The pub was quiet with everyone outside in the garden so there was no queue for the telephone. This was around fifteen years before mobile phones were a common thing, and the only one's you'd really see would be in the hands of yuppies and MPs on the television. Ronny explained to his teacher that some local lads had donated him the cash, and that he could continue with his course. The bad news for us was that Doreen Coates had heard the whole conversation.

Thursday July 16th

Mum woke me up shouting up the stairs "I've just had Doreen on the phone. How on earth have you got hold of £300?". This is all I needed, and I had to think on my feet. "What are you talking about". I said, "I haven't got that sort of money!". "Doreen said that she heard Ronny Braker speaking on the phone in the pub, telling somebody that you had given him £300." "Well, she's wrong" I said. "Well, she's telling Marie Radford as we speak." (Carters mum). "So, you two better have a good explanation." "Honestly mum, I do not have a clue what she is going on about, and now I've got to get ready for school". Half an hour later I was at the bus stop waiting for the coach to take us to school. Carter was there, Marie had taken a call from Doreen as well. Carter had told his mum that Seth had recently sold his old Fiat, and felt sorry for Ronny, so had loaned him the cash. Carter was a much quicker thinker than me, and his mum had swallowed his lie. Hopefully Marie could smooth it out with my parents too. "This does prove a couple of things, though," said Carter. "We have to be so much more careful from now on, people like Doreen are going to ruin this for us." "We've got to warn Seth not to drive his car around the village anymore too" I sniggered. "I have got an idea" Carter said. "Let's put on the biggest and best party that Danehill has ever seen." I loved Carters idea, and I was pretty sure the others would to.

We caught up the other lads that evening and explained what had happened. Pat looked concerned, which wasn't like him, but Rabbit dismissed the notion that we might get found out, which wasn't like him! This whole situation was confusing everybody, and the stress was starting to show. Seth was now worrying about driving his car. "You shouldn't be driving it anyway mate" I said, "You haven't even passed your bloody test, in fact you aren't even old enough to take lessons". It was clear that they all needed to listen to Carter – we all needed to let our hair down and enjoy yet another weekend of debauchery. Carter excitedly old them all about his notion for fun and adventure, and of course everyone was keen.

Acid House music was at its peak in 1987. Parties were put on all over the country. It was all done illegally, and the nights would get out of control. We didn't want people turning up from all over the county with smiley men faces on their t shirts. We needed to keep this small, about two hundred people. We planned on hosting an evening that all the local kids our age could enjoy and put on a party that could involve the kids who couldn't afford to get down to Brighton for the night, for kids that weren't old enough to drink in the pub, and for kids who needed some fun in their lives, away from the monotonous lifestyle of countryside living. We had friends who were heavily into thrash metal, we had friends who loved house music, we had friends who loved pop, we even knew some Goths. We wanted to put on a huge bash, but we needed to ensure that it was kept quiet. The volume of the music wouldn't be an issue but the fact that it was us organising it would. Nobody could know that we would be spending big. We didn't have access to the internet back then so we couldn't exactly invite everybody via Myspace or Facebook. We would have to alert the partygoers by word of mouth.

It wasn't hard to sort out a venue. We lived right on the outskirts of Ashdown Forest, and the hinterlands of the river Ouse. There were vast stretches of land all around us. We could easily find a spot that was out of the way of prying eyes and ears. Seth and Pat were sent off on the mopeds to scout the area beyond the former air strip to find a location. They soon returned with news that they had found the perfect place. It was about five miles from the main road but close enough for people to easily find, with access from a slightly overgrown country lane. It was called Pippingford Park and, was once a part of the army training zone. It had the fast-flowing river Ouse on one side and a dark blanket of high trees on the other. The nearest house was probably about six miles to the East, and 10 miles to the West. We all agreed that this was where the party could take place. We could build a huge fire and hire in a sound system. There would be no expense spared, and why should there be – we had the means and were more than ready to spend. Now all we needed was some guests.

We settled on a date for the bash. Saturday 18th July, coincidentally my birthday, was to be our debut as party organisers, and it had to be flawless. We invited our closest friends, that was no trouble, and they would let others know, and they wouldn't ask questions as to how we got the money together to pay for the sound system and the alcohol. We also had some flyers printed and got them passed around at other local schools and clubs. Word started to get around, and excitement was building. Rabbit had spent all his spare time up at the scene of the upcoming party finding wood and carefully building a huge bonfire. Ronny had taken his brothers tractor and helped us out by picking up the sound system and the alcohol from a nearby town. By the Friday the rest of us had all finished our school year, and so we were also on hand to help prepare and organise. The summer holidays were now upon us, and 1987 was going to be the best one yet. We were kicking it all off with the party to end all parties. We then had six weeks to spend (literally) having fun times. As mates we had achieved all this together, and there was so much more to come. There were talks between us of holidays abroad and night clubbing in London. This was going to be the best summer any of us had ever experienced.

Saturday July 18th

Today was my birthday. I was now sixteen. Birthdays obviously were always fun, and this one was no different. I felt awful when mum and dad presented me with £50. It was very kind of them, but I now had a fifth share of around £30,000 available to me when I needed it. There was also the very real notion that I had a lot more money coming to me over the next few months. We still had a lot of things to sell from our hidden collection of stolen goods and that was something we needed to act upon next. The day of the party was now upon us. We couldn't wait, and we were all at the location by noon. The excitement had got to us, and we raring to go. The country lane up to the huge fire that Rabbit had built was carefully signposted with an explanation for all guests to keep quiet on the approach. We didn't need anybody finding out about our massive soiree. Ronny had used the tractor to move away all the dry branches leaves from the area to stop the fire if it were to get out of control. We had bought some huge barrels to store bottles of booze in. We didn't want people to have to spend money on alcohol and had made it clear that all was to be provided. All people needed to bring was themselves, their closest friends, and their dancing shoes.

By mid-afternoon the party was ready to go. We had planned the whole thing perfectly. Now we had a few hours to spare. We stayed onsite and enjoyed some valuable time together. We played football and raced the mopeds at breakneck speed round and round the unlit fire pile. We were in such high spirits. Yes, we were looking forward to partying, but there was a certain satisfaction in the fact that we were doing this for others as well. We were ensuring that everybody would have a good time at our expense, and it felt good. At around six o'clock we started up the sound system in preparation of the first guests arriving. Pat and Seth visited the local record store 'Master Sound' and emptied their shelves of all the vinyl records and compact discs they could get their hands on. We had hundreds of records, CD's and tape cassettes and started to select which music we were going to play first. I felt like a superstar DJ. Half an hour later and Rabbit lit the fire. This was it – party time.

It started off so well. By around 8 o'clock there must have been around three hundred people there. We were having so much fun. The music was pumping, and people were dancing like they've never danced before. Our guests were very keen on the alcohol we had provided – who knew? Every so often I'd catch the eye of one the other lads and give him a knowing smile or a wink. We had created this, and it was going down a storm. The fire was like a beacon and had caught the attention of many more party goers from the surrounding area. As it turned out, a good few more than what we'd expected. People were arriving in their cars and parking them in a semi-circle around the fire. With their headlights on, which were catching the light of the dancing as people moved to the heavy baseline of the music, it was like a scene from an American movie.

By 10 o'clock the amount of people had doubled. Rabbit and Seth were ruling the roost, they'd positioned themselves by the fire, and in charge of the sound-system. They were playing all sorts of tunes – from Pink Floyd to Led Zeppelin, and Ozric Tentacles. I even remember them playing Peter Gabriel's Passion of the Christ album at some point. It had turned into some sort of hippy commune. Some of the new revellers were taking illegal substances and moving gently to the music like a demented version of Kate Bush – it was all very surreal. Pat had caught the attention of a few girls and was doing his best to chat them up, although by now he'd had a few drinks and even though he was sounding totally incoherent – he was telling them that this was his party - for some reason the girls were lapping it up.

There were a bunch of lads from Worsted Haynes, and even they were enjoying the party. We thought we'd have to keep an eye on them, but it was evident that it was only on the football pitch that our rivalry played out. The free booze and girls on tap were more than enough for them to put the local conflict to one side, at least for tonight. Giles Smedley had also turned up. He was with a bunch of very well-spoken friends of his and they were also making the most of the evening. A group of air hostesses had flown into Gatwick airport from Malaga that night; they had heard about the party and headed to the forest still in their Dan Air uniforms, they seemed to know the dance moves to every song going and were entertaining the masses. We had friends from the village, friends from school, and were making many more as the evening progressed. It was a real eclectic mix of people and for the most part they were sound.

Carter and I were trying to keep control of the situation, as we could see that it was only a matter of time before this all blew up. It would just need a tiny spark, and this could all get out of hand. We didn't want to be seen as the boring party poopers but always at the back of our minds we were aware of protecting our secret. We wanted to have fun, and for the most part we were but our anonymity was paramount. We did wonder whether we should have hired some local heavies to help with the security, but this idea was soon batted away, but that was before we the evening had grown so big. There were more and more people arriving who we didn't know.

And then, just like that it all turned. Carter and I had joined Seth and Rabbit by the fire. We were busy going through the pile of vinyl to find the perfect track. It was almost midnight, and we planned on a sort of New Year countdown to really get the party to the next level. That's when we saw the lights; nine or ten sets of double lights, headlights. At first, we thought we'd been rumbled and that they were police cars, and they we realised that these were no law enforcement vehicles. They were big four by four off road trucks, and they were packed full of young men – There must have been about 80 lads, and they were shouting and hollering as they left the country lane and headed over at speed towards us, and the giant bonfire. The party was in full swing, and the music was loud, so initially not everybody noticed this marauding group of trespassers.

It was soon clear that they were not here to enjoy the evening. In fact, they very much wanted to ruin ours. They stormed the bonfire, and it came crashing down around us. People were running in different directions, disorientated, and screaming. The music was silenced as one of the trucks hurtled over the sound system, it sunk into the earth beneath the huge tyres of the four by four. These lads were much older than us, they were wild eyed and drunk. A big group of them leapt off the back of the vehicles and set about throwing punches at our guests. A huge fight ensued with some of the party goers hitting back. It was absolute carnage, and they were intent on causing as much trouble as they could. It was extremely lucky that we had cleared all the dry leaves and grass from the area because a forest fire would have been on the cards, and that would have been horrific. The noise was intolerable. There were bloody faces there were people crying and shouting, injured bodies lying on the floor of the forest.

I found the others and we decided that the best thing we could do was to get out of there. We thought we could leave the area in one of the old cars we had been using for stock racing, but they were visible to our unwanted guests. My heart was beating so fast, and sweat was dripping off me, as we ran as fast as we could towards the line of trees beyond the embers of the now defunct bonfire.

And then we heard the sirens. There must have been twenty police cars converging on the forest. Everybody began desperately dispersing the area, all in different directions, the more confusion this caused, the less people would be caught and arrested by the force. But this wasn't our local copper, these were serious police. They must have been sent in from the local town. The official cars were rounding up as much people as they could, but it wasn't an easy task. The five of us were now several hundred metres from the party area and were watching this unfold safely crouched down in a large ditch. There were now people fighting with the law. The truncheons had been drawn and people were being beaten by force, they weren't taking any prisoners. We had no clue who the strangers were that had gate crashed out rave and could only assume that the police had been called because of the noise and the uproar of the party. The fire too had risen high in the air like a beacon and could likely be seen from miles around. "Well, it was a cracking do" Carter said. We all laughed, nervously. We needed a plan to get out of here. "We can't drive out now." said Rabbit. "We'll have to wait for everything to calm down and then leave." "It's not going to calm down" Pat slurred. "The old bill will be here all-night sorting this. It's a crime scene." "The cars and bikes aren't in our name's. We can leave them here and make a run for it. It's a big walk the long way round but at least we can get away without being spotted." Seth pulled up a bag from beside him. It was full of beers. "At least we've got some refreshments for the stroll." And so off we went. Cans of beer in hand, on a very long ramble that took us very much the long way back home.

Sunday July 19th

I was up early the morning after the infamous party. Mum was walking up the village to church, so I sauntered along with her. We popped into the local store on the way. "Did you hear about last night?" Mr March asked mum. "There was a huge disco up on the forest, the police had to break it all up. They arrested over 30 youngsters." Mum looked at me. I gave her the look of innocence.

"I spent the night round at Seth's" I told her. What is it about lads and their mums? They can never quite believe their brave little soldiers are capable of anything bad. I desperately wanted to catch up with the others that morning, but mum insisted I returned home and help Dad out. I enjoyed spending time with dad, always had, and we spent a good morning together. We had an old Aga oven at home, and we chopped up logs from a fallen tree in the woody area behind our house. Dad was always prepared, and he wanted to get to the tree before another neighbour had the same idea. We'd be fine for logs for the winter now. It seemed extremely organised to me and I sarcastically took the mickey out of him all morning. Sasha had been out horse riding, and when she returned home dad suggested we walked up to the Alligator for some Scampi in a basket. Mum could meet us there after church, so off we went.

The pub garden was absolutely rammed and, just like in the shop earlier, all the talk was about the 'rave' on the Ashdown Forest.

Carter was there with his old man. "Afternoon Connor" dad said. "What is all silly old chatter about then?" Connor explained the whole story to my dad. It was funny for Carter, and I were sitting there and taking it all in. Knowing that half the stuff they'd been told was absolute rubbish. But we managed to keep our mouths shut. We were grinning at each other. Connor and dad were old school. They didn't go in for gossip. They thought it was just some local lads having a bit of fun. They wouldn't admit this in front of their wives though.

It wasn't long before the local copper turned up. Nigel Sun was a decent man, a real village policeman. He would cycle round Danehill with his large belly protruding out over his belt and his trousers tucked into clips, so they wouldn't get stuck in the wheel spokes of his antique bicycle. He would keep his eye on things and make a point of visiting the local businesses every day to make sure all was okay. He'd have a pint in the pub, and always join in the local pantomimes, and singalongs at Christmas. He was a part of the furniture, just like everybody else. A real character, and fun to be around. Nigel always gave the homegrown kids the benefit of the doubt in any policing situation. But this one was serious. He said that people had been badly hurt and a massive fire had almost set the whole of the forest alight. He said that cars had been stolen, mopeds set on fire, and 45 arrests made. "There weren't enough cells in Springley Heath (The local town), so they had to cart a load of them off down to Brighton." He said, Mum then arrived and joined us she had heard all about this "Illegal rave" at church and had heard even more totally obscure and wrongful information about the evening. "Apparently there were 4,000 teenagers there" "And people were selling narcotics" she added. The village gossips had really gone to town on this one.

Later that afternoon the five of us met up over on the recreation ground. Everybody was very amused by all the stories, and great hilarity ensued as Carter, and I told them the rather loosely based on truth stories we had heard. Rabbit was concerned. "We need to find out who has been arrested because there could be some people locked up who can give our names to the fuzz". "There really isn't much we can do about that mate". I said "But even if they do give our names there isn't any proof that we had anything to do with it. We will just have to deny everything if anybody does. But I'm not sure anyone would do that to be honest. The only people we had invited ourselves were our mates, and the rest were strangers. I think we might get away with it."

Monday July 20th

It was obvious that we were running risks. The party was wild, and one for the ages but we were still not sure if we had really gotten away with it. That Monday the local newspaper ran a front-page story with all the gory details. They indicated that the police were on the lookout for the party planners, but they had no leads yet. We had heard from a couple of close friends, who were taken into custody. Apparently, the names given in as being involved ranged from Mickey Mouse to Donald Duck and Mike Yarwood. We even put in a telephone call to Eddie, to see if he could find anything out, and put our minds at rest. Eddie had laughed that we were in the big time now, and a proper bunch of gangsters. Eddie advised us not to be overly concerned, as even if somebody did give our names to the police there was no proof that we were there. We were new to this game and had a lot to learn. We had paid the deposit for the sound system in cash, and all the beer had been purchased from stores several miles away and our faces wouldn't be known to the owners.

The five of us were still trying to work out how we were going to pay for a holiday abroad without raising suspicion. There was just no way that our families would believe us if we said that we had been saving up. Flights to Europe were not as cheap as they are now, and holidays were a pricey business. We thought it might be best if we went down to the West Country for a bit of camping instead.

We sat down at a table in the pub garden in the Wagon and Ponies and started to plan our assault on North Devon and the surrounding countryside. Toggy approached our table and bought us a round of shandies. He was good like that. He knew we were under-age, but he took care of the local lads when the pub wasn't too busy. Toggy also presented us with a flyer. "Take a look at these lads" he said, "A local girl has a brain tumour, and her family need £15,000 to fly her out to America for a life-saving operation. They are looking for a sponsor but haven't got much time. She has only got weeks left, maybe even days" And that is when our plans for a camping holiday were put on hold.

"That Is all very well" said Pat "But how do we give her £15,000 without giving ourselves away?". We went through a few ideas. "How about we hold a charity event and then lie about what was raised? We could add £15,000 to the pot and nobody would know." Rabbit was clever. "That is a fantastic idea mate". I said

"But how are we going to organise that so quickly? This girl might only have days left." Carter butted in, "The obvious thing to do is to just turn up at the family's home one night and put an envelope full of cash through their letter box. But we could also use this to our advantage as well as hers…"

Wednesday July 22nd

Two days later and we were walking down the mile-long beach tree lined driveway to the massive mansion on the Larch Grove Estate. It was the biggest house for miles around, and was built in the 1500's. As we approached the property, we could sense the history. You could tell it was once a grand place, there were six tall pillars outside, and it had the look of the National Gallery on Trafalgar Square. Many ornate statues filled the garden and there was a huge maze, and a large pond that you could imagine once held hundreds of colourful Koi carp. Now however it looked unkempt and untidy, it had certainly seen better times; much like the owner's family name. England's former prime minister Sir

Harry Johnstone had agreed to see us five lads for a hastily arranged meeting. The Johnstone family had been the richest in the area, if not the whole county for some years, but their fortune had all but been lost in the recession. They liked to give the impression that they were still millionaires, but we knew better. Ronny Brakers dad had been a gamekeeper on the estate for a long time. He had got drunk in the pub one evening and let on to a few people that they weren't maybe as well off as people thought. Carter's dad had been there. He told Carters mum and Carter had overheard. This was gold.

We were greeted into the huge hallway by a Jeeves like character. He took our coats and led us into the library. Rabbit remarked that he felt like we were stepping into a game of Cluedo, and that he hoped we wouldn't get murdered with the candlestick. It had been years since anybody had seen old Harry in public, and he when he shuffled into the room to see us, it was on the arms of two men. It was clear that he was not in the rudest of health himself. He was dressed in a dressing gown and slippers and looked a lot older than his 72 years.

"For what do I owe the pleasure?" Johnstone said as he took a seat in a big comfy looking leather armchair by the fire. "I am not used to seeing the young in my house. I haven't seen a kid in here since my own boy lived here back in the 1950's." We'd been told that the former PM was not a bad bloke at all. He seemed friendly enough to us but, as a former conservative politician, and leader of our country he must have some sort of combative streak in him somewhere. We were wary but knew we held all the cards so were keen to get straight down to business.

Carter loved to read and had noted that Johnstone had once been the CEO of Sotheby's – the oldest and most respected auction house in the UK. "We've come to make a deal with you." said Carter. Johnstone was certainly intrigued. "How on earth do you propose a deal between me and you". He replied. "You are five young men in shorts. I am the former leader of this country. What on earth have you got that I will need?" "So, why did you agree to see us" Carter replied quickly. "You know as well as I do that your public persona is at its lowest ebb. And we know that the Johnstone family are skint. We can make you a deal. A deal that will make the World believe that you are cash rich. This deal will put you back in the public arena. This will in turn give you the opportunity to make some money of your own." "Continue young man" Sir Harry Johnstone was now most definitely interested.

Carter and Rabbit had concocted a story that we all believed was plausible. We told the old man that we had we had recently helped a local firm with a house clearance. We explained that we had been extremely lucky and found a mattress full of cash that amounted to around £15,000. We then said that we had unearthed an old metal trunk that was locked fast with an old iron clasp, and that the company had said we could take it away and keep whatever we found inside. We thought that the coins we had found were maybe worth some money and wanted to take them to Sotheby's for an evaluation. We preceded to explain how we wanted to help the family with the ill daughter but did not want to being attention to ourselves as the house clearance company would realise what we had done. Johnstone seemed to be buying our rather tall tale. "I can see why you need me for the Sotheby's evaluation" he said. "But how is this going to benefit me?"

Rabbit continued, "Sir Harry, we are aware that you and your family are short of cash. Luckily for you though, not many people know this. Now, we were thinking that we could donate the cash to the poor family so that this young girl can get the treatment she needs in the United States, but we will tell the press that it was you who made the donation. Everybody will think you are the hero, that you are still rich, and put you back into the public's conscience. Then we will give you 10% of whatever the coins are worth so that you can get back on your feet. It's a win, win situation, for all involved."

We were pleasantly surprised that Johnstone agreed on the spot. "He was obviously more desperate than we thought" Pat remarked as we left the mansion. We went straight round to the family home, and gave them the cash, explaining that the former Prime Minister has kindly donated the £15,000 to them, and that they could now fly out to the exclusive New York hospital to save the young girls life. They were all in tears, and we all felt great at what we had done. It was bittersweet as nobody knew it was us, but we had done some real good. We all felt that we had somehow made up for the fact that people had been beaten to a pulp at our party. By the time the evening came the generosity of Sir Harry Johnstone was being announced on the local television news. Coast to Coast (The regional news show) was camped out at his mansion, reporting live on the comeback of the former politician. The former minister looked in high spirits. He no longer looked like the guy on his last legs that we had spoken to earlier that day, he had a spring in his step and seemed ten years younger.

Thursday July 23rd

The next days Mid Sussex times newspaper was devoted to the goodwill of Johnstone and his family. This could not have gone any better for the old man. We were summoned to his mansion on the grand estate that afternoon. Johnstone wasn't around as he had been invited to host a hastily arranged charity event in London. He had left the details of a former colleague of his at Sotheby's, and his butler handed it over to us. Rabbit was overjoyed "These lying, cheating Conservatives will do anything for a bit of exposure" "And for cash!" I said, our next job was to get in touch with the auction house and plan a trip to London. Rabbit and Seth were sent off up to the Isle of Thorns to search through the hold and find the antique coins. Carter, Pat, and I wandered down to the centre of the village to use the pay phone. "Hello, is that Sotheby's…" Carter said in the poshest accent he could muster.

Monday July 27th

By 11am on Monday the 27th of July we were sat on a train from Springley Heath to London Victoria. We were sat in First Class, the first time any of us had actually paid for the pleasure. I was sitting in my seat watching the countryside speed by thinking about the past few weeks, and how much things had changed since the 100th Anniversary Weekend. We were just five lads with simple lives back then. Now we were on our way to a meeting with a top executive at Sotheby's. We had made some serious cash, we had hosted the party of the year, we had met a former Prime Minister, and made acquaintances with an ex-convict, but more importantly we had saved a girl's life.

We arrived at Victoria train station and walked across the concourse and left the station. Our nation's capital always got me excited, and I loved visiting London. Everything seemed so big, and the noise was incessant. The double decker buses, the black cabs, and the glorious mixture of people and cultures were all around you. The smells of the cafes and restaurants hit you as you strolled along the busy streets, it was an amazing place to be. I dreamed of living here one day. We entered the tube station and took the Victoria line to Green Park. It was only one stop but even in that three-or-four-minute journey there was so much to consume. A Hen party all dressed in nun's habits, a family of tourists from the USA with 'London' emblazoned across their ill-fitting sweatshirts, office workers on their way into work or hurrying to their meetings. Despite all this action, it was almost deadly silent save for the odd rustle of a newspaper or the feint sound of music from a Walkman. Rabbit kept the coins safely close to his chest in his rucksack, and almost instinctively we formed a ring around him, protecting our treasure.

As we left the underground station the rain hit us. It was bucketing down, but the sun was still shining brightly above us. There was probably a rainbow somewhere in the sky, but we didn't have time to look – we were too excited and had stuff to do. We took the short five minute to walk to New Bond Street and arrived at our destination. Sotheby's was housed in a grand building about halfway down the road. It must have been about five stories high, and the company logo adorned the green canopy above the edifice's entrance. We rang the bell and were beeped through the security door by the receptionist. We all had to give our names and phone numbers to the front desk team before being asked to go through the security gates. It was like being at an airport, and we, and all our items were scanned. We walked across the lobby, following a large security guard, he looked menacing but had a calming smile. He beckoned us to follow him into the lift. We and entered the old school artisan lift. It was the type of lift where you had to pull the metal gated door across with strength to slide them shut. Then once you started to elevate, the lifts would make a loud clanking sound, and you could see everything around you as you travelled upwards at a slow cankerous speed.

We got out at the third floor and were met a guy by the name of Charles Tallinger. Charles was the company coin and stamp expert. He took us into a room at the back of Sotheby's. It was dark and quiet, and all you could hear was the feint sound of traffic on the street below as we took our seats in front of his large antique mahogany desk. Charles explained that he was going to value the coins for us and let us know if they were worth putting up for auction. He was keen to note that, as friends of Sir Harry Johnstone, we were to be very well looked after. We told him that we had no proof of ownership, and this was simply waived away. Sir Harry had certainly come up trumps for us here. Charles reached into the top drawer of his desk and pulled out a magnifying monocle and started to carefully study the vast collection of coins from Rabbit's rucksack. "You can go and take a walk if you'd like" Charles said. "This is going to take a while." We all looked at each other and we all had the same thought. "We'd rather stay if that's okay?" Replied Carter. This might have been Sotheby's, but we weren't trusting anyone – not yet. "Then please, make yourselves comfortable gentlemen." Said Charles as he returned to his research.

We were all served sandwiches and drinks while we waited and sat there in Charles' office for what seemed an eternity. Eventually, after three hours Charles sat up and removed his monocle. "Well gentlemen. This is quite the find. I can safely say that is a very fine collection of coins you have in your possession. Some of these are over three hundred years old. Sotheby's will be more than happy to auction these off. We will sell them as one lot and will set the reserve price at £400,000. Neither of us said a word. We must have looked shocked as Charles laughed and told us that this was good news, and that we shouldn't look so scared. "There is even better news, the reserve price is the lowest we will allow them to be purchased at so you might well make even more of a profit." The auction will take place next week, so I will be in touch once we have finished to let you know the full details of your renumeration, which you can then be sent by cheque from

Sotheby's. "Is there any chance we can get the cash" Pat asked. "That is not a problem sir." Said Charles with a massive smile on his face. "It was a pleasure doing business with you" said Seth, and we all rose from our seats and shook Charles by the hand. This felt good, we felt like real dealers. But dealers with a dodgy story to tell, but I suppose that is what we were. We tried our best to look calm and sophisticated as we left the office, but it was hard not to smile, and our hearts must have been going at ten to the dozen as we entered the lift, to go down to the reception area. We forgot that everybody could see and hear us as we began the journey down, and we all cheered and clenched our fists in glory. It didn't matter, and who cared! We were going to make at least £400,000.

We left the auction house in understandably high spirits. There was to be no giant celebration as the happenings surrounding the now infamous Ashdown Forest party had put us off. We took a much more sedate stroll around Green Park and drank a pint of lager at a pub in nearby Shepherds Market. We were safe in the knowledge that we had much more money coming our way but also had lots more stuff to sell, so we still had a lot of work to do.

Thursday July 30th

The following day we were up at the Isle of Thorns. The defunct swimming pool was now a skateboard park, and Seth and Pat were going through their whole repertoire of tricks whilst the Carter and I relaxed in the sunshine. Rabbit had his driving test that day, so we all waited eagerly for him to come back with good news. It would make a big difference that we could drive around the neighbourhood knowing that we weren't going to be stopped and pulled over, especially as we now wanted to get rid of the rest of stuff we had stored at the Isle of Thorns. Rabbit was to be our delivery driver from now on. Seth had done the wise thing and sold his Fiat. At around two o'clock in the afternoon Rabbit arrived with his driving licence now legally updated, and we were good to go. Our destination was the home of Bert Hudson in Larch Grove, the art dealer that Mickey Hamble had told us of last week in the Alligator. We loaded the collection of old paintings into a hire van and sped off down the road.

Bert was a wealthy man. And as we pulled off the main road, we entered his property. His mansion house sat at the very end of the driveway. It was a beautiful old building from the 1700's. And from afar it looked like a landscape painting by Turner, like it had been deliberately placed there, it was perfect. We noted the make of the cars parked on either side. The vehicles were a real juxtaposition to his home; there was a brand-new BMW 3 series to the left, and on the other side a Mercedes Benz 500 SEL. The garage door was open and parked inside a bright red Ferrari Testarossa. This man had style. There was a lad there with long hair, who looked a bit like a surfer, and he was busy polishing the Ferrari. We recognised him instantly, and he introduced himself as Jason Cherry. Jason was a bit of a local celebrity, as he had recently won the Sussex BMX racing Championships. Jason was

Bert's handyman and lived in Worsted Haynes. He said that he was hoping to compete in the nationals if he could get some sponsorship and Carter offered him the use of the empty swimming pool at the Isle of Thorns if he needed to practice.

Bert came walking out to greet us. This man was as suave as they come. He was dressed in a lilac linen suit with hush puppy shoes and wore a big pair of Ray Ban sunglasses. He ordered Jason to collect the paintings from the van that Rabbit had hired and ushered us to the veranda. The view from here was stunning, you could see all the way to the South Downs, and the bright sunshine made it look even more impressive. In the foreground was a huge lake, that Bert said belonged to him, and beside that a large field where three of Bert's horses were standing, their tales swatting away the insects that had flown up from the lake. It was quite the scene, and we were very impressed. We sat down in some comfy chairs on the veranda and were served some chilled pink lemonade by a very pretty, young woman. We assumed this was Bert's other half. He really was a cool customer.

Bert knew his stuff. Well, it seemed as though he did. We were certainly not art experts, but as he perused the dozen pictures, he did so in a way that said to us he was an aficionado. "Listen lads, what you have here is a fine collection but if I was to buy all of these from you, I must do so in the knowledge that I'll be making some money as well, so don't expect me to pay what they are worth. I won't rip you off, but I will be benefiting myself as much as you." At least he was being honest we thought. "I can see from the state of you that you are not the owners of these lovely pictures, so I won't ask any questions either". Very fair we thought. "Don't think that I wasn't going to check you out before I met you either" He went on, "I am an acquaintance of Brighton Eddie, so I have done my due diligence, and Eddie has vouched for you all. You are lucky in that respect." "Now, I need to make a few phone calls to a few other dealers to get some more information on these paintings so make yourselves at home for a few minutes."

We kicked off our shoes, took of our t shirts and manoeuvred our chairs so that we were all facing the beautiful view. This was the life. Pat was chatting to Bert's wife and doing his best to impress her, but she wasn't in the slight bit interested. We all giggled at his audacity. "Pat, we're trying to do a deal here. You are going to ruin it if you end up fornicating with his Mrs!" Rabbit was laughing uncontrollably. "Come back over here and sit down you, silly sod".

Thirty minutes later Bert returned with a large briefcase in his hand, and a big smile on his face. "You boys have struck gold" he smirked. "These paintings are top quality merchandise." I was sweating, yes it was hot, but it wasn't the heat getting in my pores. It was the nervousness of this situation. Just how much were we going to make? This sounded BIG!

We drove the hire van back to the Isle of Thorns in a state of shock. "We are going to have to open a bank account" Carter said. "We can't" replied Rabbit. "We have to keep this quiet." Pat laughed, "We can't keep £1.2 million under our mattresses" We were millionaires now.

Friday July 31st

The Isle of Thorns was relatively safe. Nobody ever went there, and now that the school holidays were in full swing, there was always one of us onsite to take care of our new belongings, and that pile was going down fast. A huge amount of money was a different story though. We certainly couldn't afford to leave that lying around. It was a straightforward discussion; we all trusted each other implicitly, so it was just the case of working out which of our households was the most secret and work out the best place to hide our frequently growing collection of used bank notes.

Both Carter and I lived in small dwellings, we also had mothers who were at home all day. There was no way we could get away with hiding that amount of money without it getting found. Pat's mum and dad were back from their holiday but were growing suspicious of what we had been up to since they were away. The fact that several of the kennels had been tidied and shifted around had got them thinking that we were up to something, so we assumed it best to stay away from the Wishing Kennels for now. We thought about hiding it all in a water-tight container and keeping it underground or in a well but that would still be out in the open so to speak so it was down to either Rabbit or Seth's homes. In the end we decided on keeping all the money at Seth's. He had two brothers, but they respected each other's privacy and wouldn't go snooping around Seth's private belongings. His parents too were easy going and good-natured human beings. The cash, we thought, would be safest there. The fact they had a house alarm, and a large dog would also help.

We grabbed what we had left over from Eddie's cash injection and put it in the briefcase with the money we had got from Bert. We then placed that inside a securely fastened waterproof bag and dug a large hole directly behind the family summer house. Seth often slept out there in the summer so him going in and out all the time wouldn't arouse any suspicion within his family at all.

Tuesday August 4th

It had been a quiet weekend. We raided the local Halford's bike shop and spent big on five new bicycles and got out of the village. We visited a few pubs in the surrounding areas, and our very official looking fake I.Ds had been a Godsend. The weather had been beautiful, and we didn't have a care in the World. We were millionaires after all. We bought beers, sampled menus and chatted to girls. We did what any other lads our ages were doing. It was true that we were rich beyond our wildest dreams but there had been an awful lot of pressure on us these past few weeks, we had been busy making life changing decisions, we had been to important meetings with former prime ministers, we had ran from the police, and lived in a perpetual state of excitement, tension and fear all at the same time so it was about time that we lived normal lives for a while.

We spent the Monday getting over our hangovers and on Tuesday we spent the day at Carters home. His parents and sister had taken a day trip to the beach Pevensey Bay, so he had a free house. We made the most of it, and raided the treat cupboard, and drank pop from the Soda Stream. Carter's phone number was the one we had given to Charles Tallinger to contact us on once the auction was over, and we were expecting the call to come soon. I was in a thoughtful mood "Boys, how good was that feeling when we sorted out the trip to the US for that poor girl?" They all agreed that it felt great. "Maybe that should be our MO from now on. Instead of worrying about getting caught we should help people out. That way if we are found out at least we can say that we did some good with the money?" "I agree" said Rabbit, "we could do a hell of a lot of good with all this cash." "We can keep some back though, can't we?" said Pat. Carter, Pat and Seth were all on board. We would try our best to help the locals. "We are going to be like modern day Robin Hood clones" Pat said. "We can't though mate" said Rabbit, "we still need to keep this quiet." Firstly, we've come across the money illegally and secondly, we are still not sure exactly who it belongs to. They might still be on the lookout for it." Carter butted in, "So, do we just get Johnstone to pretend he's doing all of this? I can't stand the thought of that slimy Tory bastard getting all the credit. He's already back in the big time because of that poor girl. He's also getting 10% of what we make from this auction." "That's true" Rabbit stated, "Then we'll have to think of other ways of covering our tracks." I replied.

At around 4pm Tallinger got in touch. "Good afternoon master Carter. I presume gentlemen, that you are all huddled around the telephone right now?" "Yes, we are mate" Carter said in the poshest accent he could muster. We all giggled. "mate" Rabbit exclaimed with a big sigh and an even bigger grin. "I hope you are all sitting comfortably" "The coins did indeed get sold today. In the end they went to an overseas caller on the telephone. They went for upwards of the reserved price. Young men, today you are £500,000 richer. Congratulations. Cash or cheque?"

We had done it again. Half a million pounds was now on its way to us from Sotheby's, minus 10% to Harry Johnstone. "This is all going pretty well boys" Carter said as he replaced the telephone receiver "We have made over £1.5 million in total." "I best go and get my green tights out of the wash." Chortled Pat.

Friday August 7th

We all met up at the Isle of Thorns that afternoon. Rabbit was already there, on watch. He'd arranged the rest of the goods we had left to sell. It was mainly antiques – old furniture, vases and books. There were some old manuscripts that we needed to sort through later. He had been busy – all the stuff had been collated and put into piles. There was still a fair bit left and could hopefully make us some more money. We decided to keep this hidden away for now and start getting some ideas together to plan our way of offering secret goodwill to our friends and neighbours.

We made a list of people we could help. It ranged from buying new bicycles for young kids we knew who'd had a hard upbringing to donating cash to people in debt and paying off the mortgages of our parents. The two village pubs would have secret deliveries of alcohol bestowed upon them and several local people would be happy when they found out that local tradesman would be arriving to do work on their houses that was long overdue. We wanted to reward families who'd been good to us in the past by buying them holidays abroad. We even thought it would be good to donate cash for a new church roof. It was all to be done in good intentions, and we already felt rewarded at just the thought of helping people in our region. Over the weekend we made a series of phone calls. Local plumbers, painters and electricians were booked at double rate to work from Tuesday morning. They were told they'd receive the money anonymously, and that it would be delivered to their houses on Monday night.

It was decided that some of the help would have to be seen to come from Harry Johnstone, as we couldn't just leave envelopes stuffed with cash for everybody. We thought Sir Harry would be on board with sponsoring Jason Cherry in the national BMX Championships and making donations to several local charities. It wasn't ideal but he wasn't a bad man to have on board should we need anything in the future. He had already made £50,000 more from the sale of the coins and he was now back in favour with the hoi polloi of Sussex.

Monday August 10th

We began the week in good spirits. We had finished our list of people that were to benefit from our ill-gotten gains and had divided up the monies into envelopes and bags ready to deliver.

The five of us were still not completely sure of how this would go but we thought that the best way would be to secretly deliver the cash to homes under the darkness of night. We purchased some balaclavas, gloves and dark clothing, and decided to start delivering the cash that evening. Rabbit thought we looked like a smaller, and much weaker version of the SAS, but Pat kept going on about us being the modern creation of Robin Hood and his merry men. He'd bought some black tights, which he wore over his face instead of a balaclava. In all, we had £600,000 worth of cash stashed in the back of an old Bedford van we had bought from a local garage.

We waited until well after midnight, when most of the villager's bedroom lights had been turned off in their homes, and the occupants were drifting off to sleep. I loved the village at this time of night. It was so peaceful. Quiet but for the odd bit of noise from a barn owl or a fox. There were no televisions or radios on, there was no sound of laughter and no sounds of arguing. The air was still. The roads were quiet, and the church bells were mute. As a close group of friends, we had spent many nights walking this area at a late hour. Back then we had to stifle the laughter and drunken chat as we made our way across the village, loaded with cans of beer, to our camping area. Tonight, we were on a mission, and there was no need to tell each other to keep the noise down. We knew exactly what we had to do, and we wanted to do it right. In each package we wrote down the instructions of what was to be done with the money and signed them 'Robin Hood'. We hoped that the instructions would be followed.

'Operation Help Danehill' was underway, and many of the locals would awake the next day with hope in their hearts once again. It was to be like Christmas day on acid, and we were the drug dealers. We had fifty-five houses to visit in total. We would start right down at the bottom of the village and make our way up to the very top, finishing off at the church. It had all been carefully choreographed and planned. We imagined we would have it completed by 6 o'clock, just as the cockerels would begin to crow and the villagers would begin their working day.

At the bottom of the village there were few houses. It was easy enough to deliver what we wanted there without anyone knowing. The odd dog bark made us wary, but nobody stirred inside. We didn't want to use letter boxes unless we had to for fear of the noise waking the occupants so most of the money was left in bags on doorsteps or in envelopes, securely fixed under the windscreen wipers of the family car. Once we hit the council estate it would be much more difficult with houses bunched closer together and no long driveways. We turned off the engine and the lights of the van so not to bring attention to ourselves, and slowly took the car out of gear and let it roll down the street, carefully shutting the doors each time we left the vehicle and dropping off the parcels of cash as quickly and as quietly as possible.

There were more people in this part of the village who needed the cash, so it was the busiest part of the night. This was the trickiest part of the enterprise. We had to get this part done as it was full of fathers who worked long hours and who started their day early. Traditionally they were the breadwinners, and most of the mothers were stay at home mums. This was a different World to the one we live in today. For instance, I knew my dad's alarm went off at 5 o'clock every morning to get him to the local brick works early. We reckoned we would be done here by 4am so all was going to plan. We had to make deliveries here that included paying off large debts, giving kids their first ever holiday, leaving enough to people so that they could retire, and live the rest of their lives in a healthy space. We left people instructions to pay for their children's university or replace their old car that had been sitting stagnant on the street for a couple of years. We left enough for families to give their recently deceased spouses a send-off they deserved. We helped people who maybe couldn't afford to buy birthday presents for their teenagers.

There was no way we could allow ourselves to be seen. We may have been dressed to hide our faces but people in Danehill were nosey and even the slightest inclination that somebody might bring up that it was five young looking lads could bring attention to our door. We had to be discreet. We had to keep this quiet. By the time we reached the end of Oak Tree Cottages we were almost done on the estate, and that is when we almost got caught. Carter and I had just dropped off enough cash to our own homes to assist our parents in paying off their mortgages, so we were feeling very happy at this point. We had been so careful, and things were going well. But that was when things got a little tense.

We approached the last house on the street, number 128. The owner was an elderly lady by the name of Dorothy Wordsworth. Dot, as she was known to her friends and family, had a big birthday coming up. We had placed £100 in an envelope with instructions to throw herself a dress and buy herself a new dress for the bash. She was a close friend of my family, so I was especially proud of this one. I had come up with the idea, so it was left to me to place the cash on her front doorstep. As I walked up her path, I felt like I was being watched. I turned around and could see the faint flicker of a torch light a few houses down. I immediately turned and walked back down the path. I hid under the hedge to wait for the person with the torch to move away. I imagined it was one of the neighbours who owned a dog with a rather pressing matter. I'd postpone my delivery until they had walked back inside.

But as I sat and watched I realised that the person was coming towards the house. I don't think they had spotted me, but they were certainly on a mission to find out what was going on in my vicinity. I had been out and about for a few hours now, so my eyes had adjusted to the dark. I saw no lead and no dog in tow. The other lads had come to a stop further back and there was nothing they could do to help. Giving themselves away wouldn't be of any help to anybody. He shone the torch towards the bush and spoke "Whose there?" He said, I said nothing. I froze. He'd obviously seen me, but I had no choice but to stay silent. I leant back and put my hand on the wet grass and straight onto a squeaky dog toy. Now he really was sure that I was there. "What are you doing?" he said. Again, I didn't reply. "What are you up to? I'll call the police". I recognised the voice but couldn't place it. It was almost cutglass, like Charles Tallinger. Surely, he wouldn't be in Danehill? My mind was playing tricks on me.

I had to think on my feet. He was fast approaching. I could almost hear the beat of his heart, and his breathing was getting heavier as got closer and closer. Suddenly there was a great flash of light, I thought it was a lightning strike. The man turned to face the light. It was Rabbit, he'd switched on the headlights. I saw this as my chance and leapt up. The guy was in shock, transfixed by the light. As I jumped from the bush the envelope ripped and one hundred bank notes flew into the air. I ran to the van and jumped in the back. Lights from several houses then came on, the inhabitants eager to see what interrupted their sleep. The man ran out the field behind the houses, and we all drove off at high speed. We made sure we were well away from the street before stopping the vehicle. "That was close" I said panting away. I was sweating and the boys could see I was worried. "That bloke didn't stay around for long" said Pat, "he obviously didn't live there, what on earth was he up to?" Carter was calm, "Don't worry about it, he didn't see any of us, that's the main thing." We had parked near the bus stop and could survey the estate below us. There were no more lights on. No sign of the guy with the torch and no sound. "I think we got away with that one" said Carter, "Let's deliver the rest of these packages and go home". I felt like I had failed. Dot hadn't got her money. I'd have to sort that in the future. But for now, we were okay. Luckily for us the rest of the evening's escapades passed by with no dramas.

Tuesday August 11th

I was home, and in bed by 5 am, and I slept like a baby. That was until mum woke me up mid-morning. I knew why she had awoken me. I could see it in her face. She had tears in her eyes but was so happy, they were happy tears. Mum and dad explained to Sasha and I what had happened during the night; how a stranger had left an envelope of cash on top of the coal bunker with directions to use it to pay off their mortgage. "It was signed by Robin Hood" dad laughed as he told us this bit. "Mrs Milson next door had also had a visit from Robin" mum said. "We had a chat over the garden fence. She was told that she must spend it on Jane's wedding". Jane was her daughter. Of course, I knew this and had heard that the family were struggling to afford a decent do. Robin Hood had struck again! I advised mum and dad not to tell anybody about this. Sasha agreed "What if not everybody had been given cash? They'll be jealous" she said.

But nothing could stay quiet for long in this village. By mid-afternoon everybody within a two-mile radius of Danehill knew about it, and the gossips were in their element. The local shops were busy with people, some were telling others about how they had been left envelopes of money on their doorsteps, others were wondering why they hadn't had a visit from 'Robin Hood'. Curious, happy, annoyed, angry, jealousy, every sense of emotion was displayed. They were swapping stories all day. The Alligator was heaving with customers, but they were having to sit outside as workmen were in the bar doing up the décor. Word came from across the village that the same thing was happening at the Wagon and Ponies. Local tradesmen were enjoying this – they were getting pad double time to be in their local pubs, where beer was served free to them, literally on tap. There was a sense of happiness and togetherness. Even a lot of the people who had been ignored by the 'Robin Hood Gang' were enjoying themselves. It had bought the district together. The stores were soon having to shut as more labourers arrived onsite with instructions to work on the buildings. Families were seen driving off to Springley Heath to visit the travel agents and book some well-deserved vacations.

The main question people were asking was who it was that had decided to bring all this goodwill to the people of Danehill. The vicar had had nis new roof and had made up his mind that it was some sort of divine intervention. Others seemed to think that it was sort of government conspiracy, and we even heard of some saying that aliens had visited Sussex! The best thing for us was that nobody was suspecting five local teenagers of such a huge but pleasant act, and why would they? With everybody's back turned and enjoying the free beer at the village pubs; Seth managed to slip away home to fetch some money. He packed into an envelope and casually threw it over Dot's fence as he made his way back to the Alligator. Mrs Wordsworth would have her new glad-rags and celebrate her birthday in style after all.

The village seemed happy, and that was because of us and our good deeds. We felt safe in the knowledge that we had got away with it. Not one person had mentioned seeing anybody in the village that night. The only threat to unmasking us was the guy with the torch but we had heard nothing from him since. The fact that he had ran off presumably meant he didn't want to get seen either. We were concerned that the one thing that might blow all of this up was the fact that some people were genuinely annoyed that they hadn't been presented with any reward. We talked about delving back into our cash-supply and bringing the whole village onto an even keel but at this present time it didn't seem worth it. Some people really deserved what we had presented to them, others certainly didn't. Robin Hood didn't help the rich after all. There was no way we were going to give money to the wealthy or to any families that had done us or our families wrong in the past. We left them all behind and drove off down to Brighton to meet Eddie. We had yet more work to do.

Friday August 14th

By the end of the week, we were back at Sir Harry's place. "You young boys have certainly put a few cats amongst a few pigeons, haven't you?" he said as we entered the mansion. He was impressed, albeit a little put out that we hadn't given him a piece of the action. There was nothing he could do. He wanted everyone to believe it was him that had gone rogue and become the new Santa Claus, but he understood where we were coming from. He also knew that we could easily let the cat out of the bag and notify all that he had nothing at all to do with helping the poor young girl with the brain tumour.

We explain to Johnstone that we still have items to sell, and as we want to get rid of them quickly. Eddie had told us that morning that our remaining treasure was worth just under half a million pounds. But we just wanted the cash now, and were happy to make a loss, having the antiques in one place and the money in another was too stressful. Harry offered us £300,000 on the spot. The wily old fox had learnt something from his friend Tallinger. He knew he'd make a lot more when he'd sold it all, but it was best for all parties concerned if we shook on that and went our separate ways.

Monday August 17th

We all gathered around the television set at Rabbit's house. A press conference had been recorded the night before and all the locals had been persuaded to watch the 6'oclock news. Johnstone stood there looking resplendent in a new suit and greeted the press corps. He proceeded to announce that he would be standing for government once again. We were so angry. This was all our fault. Not only had we given him back his good name, but we had also encouraged him to get back on top. But the worst bit of the interview was yet to come.

Johnstone continued "It is only because of the good people of Danehill and the surrounding parishes, that I have decided to stand again. They have shown me so much love in the recent weeks and months. I hope I have returned the favour. This very morning, I received some good news from the East Coast of the United States. I recently donated a huge amount of money so that a young girl from the village could be flown across the Atlantic to receive a life changing operation on a brain tumour. I have been told that the operation was a success. The young lady is fully recovered and will fly home in a few weeks, once she is fully rested and recuperated. I plan to hold a huge party for her and her family when she touches down on British soil once more, and everybody will be invited. I think we should celebrate what can be done when somebody wants to really help the less fortunate among us"

Johnstone looked into the camera as it zoomed in on his face "I feel like a modern-day Robin Hood" he said as he winked at the lens. We were in total shock. We looked at each other in disgust. Pat was fuming, "I'm gonna kill him." "I can't believe that two-faced old bastard." said Carter. "He's taken the credit for everything now."

It was true, we didn't want people to know what we'd been up to, but we didn't want him to keep benefiting from our good work either. We thought we'd had an agreement with him. "I suppose it's true" Rabbit said. "Never trust a Tory". He had us over a barrel, he knew that we were never really going to expose him over the fake donation he supposedly made. It was always going to come back and bite us. "We are just going to have to suck this up" Rabbit continued "There is nothing we can do – for now. Maybe later down the line we can get him back. I suppose the saving grace is that we still have just over £1 million at our disposal."

We all thought we deserved something special seeing as though we were really the Robin Hood characters who had done so much to help the people of the village. We went out and spent and spent big. Why wouldn't we have been rewarded like everybody else? We bought a brand-new BMW, estate and that was now to be our official mobile. Rabbit would be the driver, and the rest of us would be driven around the local watering holes. It was only a couple of weeks before we had to go back to school and college, so the plan was to make the most of that time to enjoy a bit more of the money before life got boring again. None of us really knew what the future held. We decided that the best thing was to keep hold of the rest so that we could all have a decent start to adult life. We contacted Eddie in the hope that he would help us make some decent investments. It sounded boring but Rabbit and Carter saw this as the best way forward. We all agreed. We each now had just over £200,000 each for our future. We would use the 'Robin Hood' excuse if people asked us why Rabbit was now driving such a lovely car.

Thursday September 24th

The next few weeks dragged on as we got back into the monotonous hamster wheel of school life. Up out of bed at seven, at school from nine until three, homework, a bit of football in the park, TV and then bed. We were living just the same life as any other teenagers in the country. Three of us were now into our last year of school, Carter, Pat and I had a big year ahead with O Levels at the end of it. Seth was the year below and Rabbit had started his A Levels at the 6th form college in Springley Heath. The only saving grace of it being September was that the football season began once more, so I could get back on the pitch.

That night dad came home from work early. He said he had seen in the local newspaper that the Parish Council plan to reopen up the Isle of Thorns as a swimming pool for the neighbourhood kids. It wouldn't be happening until next summer, but they would start to clear the area over the next few months. I decided to visit there that night to clear out the rest of our bounty. There were just a few old diaries and manuscripts to sort through. It wasn't a huge amount, but we still needed to clear it away and get rid of it before it was found. Rabbit agreed to drop me off there, and by 9pm I was sat in a dark room with just a torch and a load of old papers for company. It wouldn't be an easy task, but I figured that it might be some worthwhile research for my ongoing school history project. My schoolwork has taken a bit of a back seat over the past few months and the last time I had done anything towards the project was back in June during the village weekend. I'd discovered that the village was just one hundred years old. I was hoping that maybe I'd get some interesting insight into village life back then. It might even be of some use to the local historical society. It would be great to report back to the chairman with something new, and it also gave me something to think about rather than money and former prime ministers.

The light outside was fading fast and there was no electricity on site. I was hidden away in an open changing room by the huge municipal swimming pool. The only light I could use was a beam of moon light shining through the giant stone pillars that held the room up. In front of me was a massive pile of paperwork. I turned on the torch and started to sort through the manuscripts. I found some old bills and receipts, some that dated back as far as the late 19th century. They were mainly bills for stuff such as animal feed and cart hire. There were also diaries from the early 1900's. I recognised some of the surnames – they were probably ancestors of families that still lived in the village. Barnyard, Damsell, Braker and Milson were commonplace on both invoices and paperwork alike. A large trunk that we must have ignored previously caught my eye. It was sat under a huge stack of old cardboard folders. It looked quite modern and was locked with a large rusty padlock. I fetched a hammer from Seth's toolbox and used all my strength to bring it down hard several times and smash open the lock – it took all the power I could muster, but eventually it smashed to bits. I opened the trunk carefully and a rancid and pungent smell instantly left the confines of the trunk and wafted into my nostrils. It was disgusting but I wasn't turning back now. The smell was familiar to me, it was damp induced, and I hoped that the papers inside hadn't been affected. They were a different colour to the rest and much older.

On top of the paperwork was some sort of pamphlet bound together with string. The string was weak and fell apart as soon as I lay my hands upon it. The papers were an off brown colour like they'd been stained by a spilt cup of coffee. I recognised the language immediately. I had studied Latin for one term at school and could see the transcript was written in some sort of medieval Latin language. It was the Domesday book, that was clear. I had also studied that in history class and to be honest, had found it quite boring, but this was now interesting me a great deal. One of the only things I remembered from that class was that the Domesday Book was written in the late 11th Century. The chairman of the historical society was wrong; Danehill had existed a long time before 1887. I needed to do more research here, and there was a lot more paperwork to go through. This was huge news. I wanted to scream and shout and let everyone know. I had made a massive discovery. I wanted to contact Phil Lomas straightaway, but there was so much more stuff to go through. I placed the Latin wordings to one side and continued to search.

There was another pile beneath the Domesday copies. They were old broadsheet newspapers from the seventeen hundreds and were contained in a very modern looking transparent A3 plastic folder. In the same folder was some very old looking journals. The journals were dated 1487, 1587, 1687 and 1787. I thought I'd better settle in for a night of exploration. This was going to take some time. For the first time in a while, I completely forgot about our situation and went into a keen schoolboy mode again. I felt that I had found out something about the village that nobody else knew. Forget Robin Hood and his band of merry men, I was the new Indiana Jones!

The diaries were all very different. They were uneven sizes, and, from the state of them, I can see that some once belonged to children, and others to adults. They were written with distinctly differing writing, and even dialect, and by names unknown to me, in fact none of them match villagers' surnames from 1987. I decided the best way was to start with the earliest journal and make my way forward. I opened the 1487 edition. It had been relatively well preserved considering it was now 500 years old. The name on the cover was Mia Proudfoot, and it stated her age as nine and a half. Much of the text was very childlike, telling how she *'helped mother with the cooking'* or *'played on the moor'*. She had also included drawings, which seemed to have been made using charcoal. The art was impressive. I wasn't really learning too much about the village save for a mention of King Edward visiting a nearby town. She also writes about the War of the Roses, and the battle of Bosworth Field. Interestingly she wrote about fishing with her brother on a *'large dangerous river that ran through the central part of Danehill'* I had never heard of any type of river being part of the villages landscape. Strangely she mentioned a battle with the people of Worsted Haynes too – Things never change.

I flicked my fingers through a few more pages and realised that they went blank from July 7th onwards. The final insert she had made to the diary was a drawing that resembled a large puff of wind, and the words *'There is a typhoon on the* way' This truly saddened me. To think that this was the final writing from this girl. Was she killed by the typhoon? Did her family survive? I had all sorts of questions. I hoped that the next diary – one hundred years on - would give me some answers.

The 1587 diary was very grandly titled *'The 1587 Diary of Sir Terrence Faraday.* It had some sort of prologue *'Dear diary, we left Scotland after the beheading of Mary Queen of Scots and travelled South to England. We are now living in a newly built village by the name of Danehill. The Elizabethan property we call our abode is on a large Estate where the deer run and the salmon leap. England is much more beautiful than I first dared to think'* There were absolutely no words describing a typhoon or the people that came before him. It didn't make any sense to me whatsoever.

He then proceeded to go on about *'hunting the wolves on the estate'* and *'courting the most wonderful women'* and *'dancing the night away at the Ashdown ball'* In the September of 1587 he scribed about *'incessant down-pours'* and *'a lake that is close to overflowing'*. Once again, the diary failed to reach December 31st. In fact, there was nothing else written after March 18th.

I took out the next journal, from 1687, out of the A3 folder. The prose was written down by a John Sutton, but there was only seven pages penned, before it went blank again. John writes about *'a snowstorm and bitter coldness in Danehill.'* The next paragraph dated 7th January sent shivers down my spine.

'As we sit in the darkness of the scullery, in this new home, in a new parish, in a new land. It is as though Danehill is cursed as just a furlong away we see it coming. The land is breaking up, it is like a biblical storm. We are not much longer for this perilous World; an earthquake is on its way.'

This was getting very weird. There was just one diary from each century in the folder, each one describing a tragedy in the village where I come from. But none of them mentioned anything about life before their diaries begin. It was as if life in Danehill only started the year their writing commences. I dreaded to think what the final two journals had to offer. I was also getting worried, as each of the writings come from a year ending in 87. This year was the year of our lord 1987. I continued with my research.

I didn't bother reading the next diary from January 1st. It was by an eleven-year-old by the name of Arlo Sussex. It ended on St. Georges Day - April 23rd, so I start perusing his words from the 16th of that month.

'16th April 1787. I am worried. It is very hot, and every day the water in the reservoir gets lower. There is no way this can be. Father says it was built just last year.'

'18th April 1787. Mother passed today. Father is not well. I here from the village elders that there is no water left. We are all going to die if help does not arrive.'

'20th April 1787. Father has gone. The drought has taken hold of the whole village. There are not many of us left.'

'23rd April 1787. I can't go on like this. My throat is dry. I am so very weak. I'm all alone.'

The final diary was from 1887 and was by a baker's wife, Jennifer Connor I flicked through the pages, taking in what I could, as I raced towards the impending doom I had now come to expect on the final page. She wrote about Queen Victoria's Golden Jubilee in the June and the street party in Danehill. 'I have been baking for weeks on end, and today it has arrived, our first party on the streets of Danehill to commemorate the Golden Jubilee of our Queen.'

But after that date it became very dark.

'July 3rd, 1887. I have read stories about the bubonic plague from many years ago. I have read that people would ride a horse and cart down your street yelling "Bring out your dead". But now that is very real for me.'

'July 7th, 1887. This plague is horrific. There are not many people left living in the village. Last night somebody burnt down the church. People are losing their minds. I am worried for my family. We want to leave but all roads from the parish are guarded day and night by these horrible creatures, they call themselves the Helpers. We are living in seems like a grave. There is no way out and we are being left to die.'

'July 12th, 1887. Today I wrote a letter to Aunt Maud in London. I yearned to tell her of our troubles. I am not sure anybody from the outside World know what trouble we are in here.'

'July 20th, 1887. My husband lost a leg this afternoon. But no doctor can enter the village since Doctor Cranston died of this very plague just two eves back.'

'July 23rd, 1887. The plague has taken hold of me. I fear my life will be at an end by nightfall.'

After that of course there are no more words. It was what I had come to expect from those diaries. It still made no sense to me at all. I was also extremely worried about what it meant for our future. Maybe we were meant to find these books? Maybe we were meant to rob the village hall and bring to light these awful goings on? I kept searching through the paperwork in the folder.

There was a newspaper clipping from page five of the New York Times, dated 12th September 1954, it was by a journalist called Chester Firmington and a paragraph was highlighted:

'I have seen these diaries. Inside them they chronicle how everyone hundred years, the small village of Danehill in West Sussex, England is overcome by tragedy. It is written that everybody in the village dies or is killed. When rescuers show up there is no belongings, no people, no bodies – nothing is left. I have spoken to various English historians, but they all dismiss this as a tale from the bogeyman. They say that the first record they have of a village called Danehill is from October 1887. Apparently before then it was just a swamp. Maybe I am reading too much into this. Maybe I am an adventurist who just loves a good story, but I'd love to know if this really rings true. And if they aren't then who on earth came up with these complex stories in these make-believe journals?'

There was also a clipping from the Mid Sussex Times dated 1961. It said similar things but, once again, they were rubbished by experts and historians alike. Maybe the chairman was right, and there wasn't a village on this site before 1887. But then why was there a mention of Danehill in the Domesday Book? I imagined the journalists weren't party to this information at the time they wrote the articles. I packed up the papers and started the long walk home in the dark. This was something I needed to discuss with the others.

Friday September 25th

Sir Harry Johnstone was still the talk of the town. Most of the locals were behind him and saw him as some sort of angel. He had certainly played us and was now playing the part. He had been busy in the press, and on the television selling himself, and his party. There was no doubt that he was going full steam ahead on his standing for government. There was even talk of the current

Prime Minister, Margeret Thatcher visiting him at the Larch Grove Estate.

I summoned my four friends. We all met up in the garden of the Alligator that night. It was quiet. The Royal It's a Knockout was on the tele, it seemed to be the highlight of the year, so most people were at home watching that. We were always close but this whole experience had bought us all even closer together. There is a bond that goes way beyond friendship. There is a certain trust, and I knew that they would back me up on whatever I said. Most people would listen to this tale and take it with a pinch of salt. But these lads would get behind me on this one, I knew that for sure.

We all sat around the table furthest from the door of the pub. It was a quiet part of the garden, where the kids play area was. It was after 9pm so no children were around to interrupt our conversation. We'd done the usual, and purchased a bottle of spirits, which we added to the lemonade we had got from the bar.

There was a short discussion regarding Sir Harry, and we all decided that he would eventually pay for taking all the credit from our good work. We weren't sure what we would do, and that would be something to explore further down the line. I then went onto explain all about the manuscripts, the diaries and the paperwork. I told them about the years with '87 in the number. They were shocked and a little concerned. "Christ Alive" Carter says, "This isn't looking good for a Happy New Year is it!" "That's if we get to New Years Eve" replied Seth. "That was my point: Carter exclaimed. "What does everyone think we should do then?" I asked. "What can we do?" Rabbit said. "Nobody will believe the stories." "But Sam has got the proof" Pat said. "We should go and see Eddie. He'd know what to do." "That's nuts" I said. "Eddie is an ex-con. I know he's been helpful to us, but I'd rather take all the papers to Nigel Swanson. That way it's in the hands of the police. Then they can decide what action to take next." "But how do we say we got our hands on it all?" Rabbit asked. "Let's take it to the historical society. They won't ask about where we found it. They'll just be happy to have a load more stuff to talk about at their monthly meetings!" "That's all very well "I said "But I'm more worried about some disease spreading the village and finishing everyone off before the years out!" "At least he can tell if it's kosher or not" Rabbit said. So, it was agreed, we'd pass on the information to the Historical Society Chairman and let him take on the responsibility.

Tuesday September 29th

The following Tuesday evening Rabbit and I went to visit Phil Lomas. Phil was a lovely old man and was Chairman of the Danehill Parish Historical Society. Phil lived in a lovely little cottage at the bottom of a country lane on the edge of the village. The lawn was perfectly manicured, and you could tell he spent an awful lot of time in garden. The summer colours of the flowers looked mesmerising in the evening sun. Phil greeted us at the door and ushered us through into his study. Inside it was a completely different story. The study wasn't tidy at all, it was as though somebody else lived inside who was so very different to the man who tended his outside space so carefully. Phil went to the kitchen to put the kettle on whilst Rabbit and I took a seat. We had to move old books and documents to make enough space to take a perch. My eyes scanned the room, three of the walls were packed with shelving from floor to ceiling, and on each shelf was a whole host of historical books and pamphlets. It was evident that he was passionate about history, and the history of the village where he had lived for all his 85 years particularly.

Phil soon returned to the study with three cups of tea and a plate of Jammy Dodgers, which he beckoned us to sample. "So, young Sam, how is your school project moving along then?" he politely asked. "Well, that's sort of why we're here" I said.

We then spent the next thirty minutes or so explaining to Mr Lomas about our find. He sat there enthralled by the tale. "Well boys" he said "This is certainly an interesting lot. The Domesday book entry is amazing. I am so surprised. If this is proved as genuine then you may have made a real find here. This could bring about so much exploration into the history of Danehill. The Historical Society might end up having a very busy year. Can I please ask where you found all of this?" I was flummoxed. Luckily Rabbit took control of the situation. "It was left on my doorstep on the night of the infamous Robin Hood escapade" he said rapidly. I was in awe of how he had thought of an answer so quickly. Phil then explained how he needed to take the manuscripts and the newspapers to some experts in Brighton, as he wanted to check the authenticity of them. We had complete faith in him, but we must have looked concerned; We must have sounded worried as he said he'd get it done quickly. He tried to put our minds at rest over the horrible situations spelled out in the diaries. "From what I can see the Domesday book looks very real indeed, but I wouldn't be at all surprised if the diaries are a hoax. Some people can be awful human beings you know. Please don't worry, this will all get sorted out. You will be heroes in the eyes of the Danehill Parish Historical Society. We might even give you both medals."

Monday October 5th

We were now on half term. And the five of us could spend some quality time with each other. There was still no news back from Phil Lomas. We didn't want to pressure him, and there had been no information about plagues, murderers, wars or floods on their way to obliterate the people of Danehill. We didn't want to alert our neighbours to any issues that may or may not happen on the future. This would either just cause panic or lead people to think we were all idiots. We had all invested a fair bit of money (We hoped wisely) via connections of Eddie and had held back some money to enjoy when we could. There was only two and a half months left of 1987 so the threat of something happening to the village and its inhabitants was decreasing by the day – At least that is what we all hoped! The only thing we could do was to wait on Phil Lomas to get back to us. We were going to have a fun week. The rest of the village were still enjoying their gifts of cash, so we felt safe in the knowledge that, so far, we had been doing the right thing.

Tuesday October 6th

There was a certain sense of freedom now that we had our own car to drive around in. There were no awkward conversations with Rabbit's parents about borrowing their vehicles. We were free to do what we wanted when we wanted. On the Tuesday we drove down to the coast and visited the town of Rye. We had spent some time down there on a camping trip previously and knew the area well. We visited pubs and shops spending money on stuff we didn't need. We stayed overnight in a little bed and breakfast place. It all felt very grown up, and having our own baths and toilets felt very different to the communal shower block we had experienced on our last visit to this old historic town.

Wednesday October 7th

On the journey back home, we stopped off at a 'Happy Eater' restaurant and, over our hamburgers and fries, discussed what our next port of call of would be. We all agreed that we wanted to help people again and decided to put on an event for the younger kids of the village. We were old hands at party organising now after all. This time there would less alcohol and music, and hopefully no sign of brawls and visiting police officers!

Friday October 9th

Friday was the final day of our short break from school, and the day we decided to host the party for the children we knew in the village. We had been out and about the day before, delivering flyers through the letter boxes of all the youngsters we thought deserved an afternoon of fun. We had signed the flyers with the now famous signature of the local hero, Robin Hood, inviting them all to a galaxy of fun on the local playing fields. By two o'clock the sports pavilion was full of eager kids. We had laid on a feast of sandwiches, sausage rolls, cakes, chocolate and fizzy pop. The five of us were dressed up as clowns and were making the kids laugh by squirting water at them, staging falls to the floor and tripping each other up. Rabbit was making some artistic balloon animals, which we never knew he was capable of. Seth played music on his CD player, and the young party goers danced and laughed away. Jason Cherry visited the party and performed some tricks on his BMX. The kids were mesmerised and stood back in amazement as this local celebrity and his skills with his bike. They all asked for autographs, and had their photographs taken with him. Once again it felt good to be giving something back to our community. After a couple of hours, we handed the children back to their parents. They were very thankful, and we, and Robin Hood, of course, were complimented with high praise.

Saturday October 10th

We continued our mission of good will to our friend and neighbours over the weekend. We invested in some car washing gear and went round the village offering people a free car wash and polish. We also purchased a whole selection of ready meals from the local supermarket and handed them out to the elderly and infirm.

Sunday October 11th

It had been a fun (And rewarding) seven days, and as I sat with my family watching Bullseye on the television on the Sunday night, I looked back at my half term week with a certain amount of pride. Not only had we had some fun together, but we had also done our bit for the locals. If this was to be the last months of Danehill's very being, then we yearned for the Danehillians to go out in style, and a happy state. We didn't know at the time but In a few days, there would be more people who needed our help, and this time not only their homes but also their very-existence would be at risk…

Thursday October 15th

By mid-October the weather had turned. We were back at school after a week off and it was all a bit depressing. I was sat in my geography class looking out of the dirty window. I couldn't concentrate at all in class and was in a World of my own. This was an important year for my studies but all I could think about was the money and the supposed fall of Danehill. The hail was coming down in biblical proportions, bouncing high off the ground, and making one hell of a din as huge droplets made a ricochet back off the classrooms window glass. The last few months had offered great excitement and now life seemed a little boring. This awful weather wasn't helping matters either. At dinner break I met up with Seth. He was of the same mindset as me. We called Carter over and instigated a meeting with the others that night. There was still a whole load of paperwork and books that we could go through, and we may have got some more clues to report back to Phil Lomas with.

We all returned to the Isle of Thorns. Five lads, with five torches and a crate of strong lager. The rain was really coming down now and the open changing room wasn't an ideal place to sit, but it was all that we had. It was the type of rain that comes at you brutally from the side and can give you a headache. We nestled against the seating area. There were three large high-backed benches which gave us some amount of cover from the heavy rainfall. I had emptied the trunk on my last visit but there was lots of extra correspondence for us to study. Most of it consisted of more invoices and bills, with a few receipts thrown in. There were love letters and shopping lists, army papers and proofs of ownership to various bits of land around the parish. But nothing jumped out at us which would assist in joining the dots in the mystery of the 'disappearing village'.

The time moved rapidly on, and the rain eventually subsided. We all felt that this was becoming a lost cause, and that we may not find a thing to help us in our research.

In fact, it wasn't until after 10pm that Seth spotted a letter. It was a very old hand-written text. The colour of the paper was a brownish yellow. The names between the two correspondents had faded through time, and some of it had been ripped at the sides but the bulk of the letter was intact. It had been written by ink and quill, and there were several blotches of ink splashed on different parts of the pages Seth began to read:

Dear so and so,

I trust this letter finds you well and at peace with our World.

I am sorry to have to write you this letter. As I sit in my garden on the most heavenly of summer evenings in the year of our lord 1886, it feels very wrong to have to write such correspondence, a letter of warning to you and your kin. The sound of the birds in the trees in my garden have done no wrong, neither the rabbits who jump and hop around the meadow behind my house. But I am sorry to say that they, as I, might one day soon perish.

As you know I am now too unwell to be able to travel by cart. The doctors fear if I do then I will not make it as far as the boundaries of the county of Sussex. Because if I could then I would be with you already.

I have discovered some awful news, of which I want you take to the authorities. I am truly hoping this letter gets to you this time. I have written this exact same letter to you before but have heard nothing in reply.

The fact is my village, the village of Danehill is under an awful threat. I have been privy to conversations between the village elders. Conversations that I should not have heard, but I am glad I did. Although perhaps not, perhaps it would be better if I didn't know of my impending doom. It seems that the village elders are not real humans. They are a group of witch-like people. They are evil and they want everything that we own. All they are interested in is money and power.

They have been planning a cull of the people of this village. They appear every hundred years and feast on the dead. They first arrived here in 1487 and fell in love with Danehill. But they were treated as outcasts. So, they took revenge on the locals. They bought forth a typhoon on the village, which killed every person in the parish. They plundered all the belongings of the dead, and then returned to hibernation, stronger and richer. They sleep for one hundred years and keep returning. In 1587 they killed everybody by creating a flood of massive proportions. In 1687 an earthquake took hold of Danehill. In 1787 a terrible drought bought the people of the village to their knees. They keep returning from their sleep every century and get more money and more strength. They hide all their treasure beneath the centre of the village.

One day they will return and take it all and live like Kings. But it is only they that will live, as I fear the people of the village will never beat them. We have witnessed the death of just one, but that was only because of too much mead. These demons seem to survive no matter what.

I have heard that a plague of rats has been released in the village, and so I now know the fate of me and the other villagers. It is written that in 1887, that is how we will be the next to die.

Please help us.

Your faithful friend,

So and so

We all took some time to take it all in. I gulped and Rabbit shook his head. Seth was first to break the silence "Well, let's hope tonight's storm doesn't come back lads." Right on queue there was a massive rumble of thunder, and the rain started again. We all looked at each other in shock, but a knowing shock. I trembled in my seat. It was incessant, hard rain. It made such a sound on the tin roof of the changing rooms. We could hardly hear ourselves think, and there was lots of thinking to be done.

Pat asked Seth to repeat a certain part of the letter *'They hide all their treasure beneath the centre of the village'*.

We now knew who the owners of all the antiques were. The treasure belonged to a load of evil witches. "That has got to be a load of old bollocks surely?" said Carter. "Come on, who would believe that load of old clap trap?" 'But it all adds up mate." said Rabbit. "The diaries, there were only five saved, and each one spoke of the ensuing terrors. The newspaper articles too. People have obviously found out about all of this is in days gone by." "So, then why has nothing ever been done?" I said "Well, let's be honest" Rabbit replied "They were probably killed. This was why there was never any record of Danehill before 1887. I am very worried now."

We all were. It was obvious that we had stolen the treasure. It was also apparent that the witches didn't want this news getting out, and anyone who knew was shut up or even killed. And now there was a massive storm taking control of the skies above Danehill. We thought it best if we all returned home. We would arrange to meet Phil Lomas tomorrow, collate all the paperwork, and take it to the police. This storm could be the start of something, something that could end up killing us all. This weather could be the work of the witches. I just wanted to get home to my family now. They were all that mattered.

I got back home at around midnight. Dad was livid. "Where have you been? The weather is absolutely atrocious. That wind is really picking up. It's getting dangerous." He said he'd been trying to ring around, but the phone lines were down. He'd been down the road to see Carter's mum and dad and almost got blown over into a neighbour's garden. I told him that we had all been round at Rabbit's. He alerted me to the fact that somebody had called in to the BBC weather. Apparently, the weather presenter, Michael Fish, had told the nation that they need not worry, there was nothing wrong. We certainly got the impression that he might have been wrong on that score. I was worried. Was this the 1987 curse? Were we all going to die in our homes tonight? Was this the hurricane that ended the latest lives of the people in Danehill? I wanted to contact the other lads, but dad was right; the phone lines were down. I'd have to ride this one out with my family. The torrential rain and strong winds thankfully subsided, and we all decided to get to bed. My head was spinning as it hit the pillow. The letter we'd found sounded ludicrous, but it was still scary. Witches hibernating and feasting on the dead! It sounded like a James Herbert novel. I didn't know whether to tell the family what

I knew but, as the weather had cleared, I thought it wise to keep it to myself for now, and I eventually fell to sleep.

My slumber didn't last long. At around 4.30am I was awoken by a loud bang, the wind had blown so strongly through the eaves of the roof and down the chimney, that the loft hatch had come loose and fallen to the floor of our upstairs landing. The four of us all came to immediately. Mum and dad ran to our bedrooms to check we were okay, and decided it was best if we were all downstairs, together. We all made our way down to the sitting room and huddled on the sofa. The noise of the whistling wind was deafening. It seemed to whirl around the whole house, inside and out. Sasha was worried about her menagerie of pets in the garden. Dad made the decision to go outside in the storm to grab her rabbit's and guinea pigs and bring them into the safety of the brick walls around us. The site of him venturing outside in his dressing gown and pyjamas to rescue my sister's pets in the middle of a pulsating storm would have been funny had it not been so dangerous. Luckily, he and the animals made it back inside in one piece. We spent what was left of the early hours of the morning sat together comforting the animals. I was not an animal lover, but they meant so much to Sasha, so I was more than happy to help. It felt reassuring to me that we were all together at this time. Once again, I felt it best not to say a thing about what I knew. My family wouldn't have believed it anyway, and I didn't want to worry them more than they already had been on that night.

Friday October 16th

By the time the sun rose on Friday the 16th of October 1987, I felt much more at peace with the World. We are still alive. I was right not to have told my family about the letters, and the diaries. Had the witches failed in their disaster that they had bestowed on the village? Was it just coincidence that a great storm had hit the village that night? Or did they have more unearthly perils to bring down upon us?

I wondered up to my bedroom window. The scenes outside looked like they'd come from a disaster movie. The wind had now calmed but the devastation it had left behind was astonishing, A neighbour's greenhouse had embedded itself in the middle of the road, and several cars were upturned. I could see smashed windows in the flats opposite our house, and trees had fallen. I could see the trunks that had been ripped from the ground. Trees that were probably hundreds of years old were now lying in the graves that their own plummet had created. I recognised some of the locals walking round in shock, taking in the wreckage. I don't suppose any of them had had much sleep, and they looked like zombies. I just hoped that everybody had survived the hurricane. There was a smell in the air, it was like rotten eggs, a sulphuric aroma that filled my nostrils as I opened my bedroom window. I called out to Norman Milson, our next-door neighbour. Norman had a CB radio and had been in touch with other handlers around the county. He told me that the whole of the parish was now cut off from the rest of the World. He had heard that the wind had reached 120 miles per hour in some places. Mum had asked him to see if he could contact any CB enthusiasts in Worsted Haynes, as she wanted to know of my nan was okay, he said he'd report back as soon as he could.

We heard that a get-together had been called in the Memorial Hall later that day. It would take a massive undertaking to clear the village, and to ensure that everybody was okay in the area, and we would all have to come together as one. The meeting would be paramount to this. In the meantime, myself, dad, Carter and Connor decided to walk the village, and try to get some indication of exactly what we were dealing with. We passed many people on the way, and heard horrible stories of pets being killed, cars rolling along the street, and chimney pots falling onto gardens. We tried to stroll through the wood, but the whole area was ripped apart. Hundreds of trees had fallen and blocked our route through.

Carter and I hung back a bit to catch up. We had to keep our conversation to a whisper, "Do you think this was the witches then? I said, "If it was then their plan didn't work" Carter agreed "The village and all of us are still here so fingers crossed. Mind you, they might have something else up their sleeves." "Come on you two" Connor interrupted our little chat. "We've got a long way to go yet." We had to turn back after a while, as there was just no way through. We could see on the streets that many trees were lying dead, blocking the roads. There didn't seem to be a way in or out of the village. We were shocked to see a horse trotting gingerly through the village; it must have escaped it's stable during the storm but there was nothing we could do to help for now. The four of us managed to get home in one piece and said our goodbyes. Dad and I went inside and could see that mum had been busy. We had an aga, so not having any power wasn't going to stop her – she'd been busily cooking up meals for the neighbours who were less fortunate. Sasha was sat downstairs still comforting her pets under candlelight. We find out in despatches that most of the South of England had been hit by the storm. If this had been the witches, then it seemed that they had massive plans this time around. If they could have looted every house on the South coast, then the money and belongings they would have claimed would have been huge. I was thinking that they had underestimated the humans of the twentieth century. We, and our homes, were now much more resilient to their powers.

That evening we made our way up to the village hall to join everybody at the meeting. It would be strange going there, since this was the place where our whole adventure had begun. I wondered where we would be now, had we not committed the burglary. Maybe I'd be more at peace, I would be totally ignorant to the fact that the hurricane had been anything to do with the witches, if indeed it had. But then again, maybe it was better to be prepared. I was hoping to see the other lads at the meeting, as we might think it better to let the locals know what we now knew. On our way up the street, we bumped into Mr Milson who put mums mind at rest. He been in touch with my Uncle Trevor, and she was fine. He said he'd organise for us all to have a chat with her on the CB radio at some point soon.

We entered the hall, and it was packed to the rafters. I remember thinking that I hoped the stage wouldn't fall in. Ronny Braker had done a good job in mending it. He'd placed some strong wooden planks beneath the floor of the stage but there was a huge empty cavern below it now and you would not want to fall through. There was a busy hum of voices, with everyone describing their own woes from the previous night's events. But the main thing was that we, and the village were still standing.

The meeting started, and it was obvious that we were going to fight on. This storm was not going to defeat us. It was decided that the telephone exchange was to be one of the first things mended, so that at least we could be in communication with the outside

World. People volunteered to help clear the trees at the end of the village where the easiest route into the nearest town was. It wouldn't be quick but at least people felt like they were doing something to help this horrible situation. It wasn't just food that people required, there were medicines, bandages, petrol and many other things that needed providing. One of the guys in the village was a worker at a company who supplied generators for big events, and he had donated a second hand one to keep at the village hall. This location was to be the hub where locals could gather and eat hot meals. The elderly would be taken care of, and anyone else who wanted could come here, even if it was just for a chat. The plan was to bring us all together as a community. As usual, our fighting spirit was second to none. The generator was already going, and hot drinks and soup were given out to all who had attended the meeting. Both the local landlords had arrived with supplies. The adults of the village made sure they had a relaxed evening after this. Others had bought musical instruments, and it turned into a bit of a party. They needed to let their hair down after an awful twenty-four hours.

Carter and I spotted the other three lads and went over to see how they were. We remembered it was Pat's birthday and wished him all the best. He told us how he slept right through the hurricane and didn't even notice that a huge branch from a tree right outside the front of his house had smashed right through one of the windowpanes in his bedroom. It wasn't the best way to celebrate his birthday, but he was just happy to have survived the incident with the branch. Him and his family had spent the day looking after the dogs who'd been in residence at the Wishing Kennels.

Rabbit had had an eventful night and day. He'd driven back from our sojourn at the Isle of Thorns and had to desert his brand-new car. He'd only got as far as the pub when he realised that the roads were blocked by fallen trees. He'd managed to lift himself over the many broken branches and make it to his homestead. Once he got there, he saw the state of his parent's garden. Another car had veered off the road and smashed through the fence. Luckily the driver was okay but his vehicle, and the garden were ruined. The family had spent the day trying to tidy it all up. They had taken the driver in, as he lived twenty miles away, and had nowhere to go.

Seth was his usual laid-back self about the episode at his house, and when he told us the story we were horrified. He, like us all, had got back late from our evening of researching and had set up camp in his summer house. During the early hours of the morning the little wooden hut almost lifted off the ground. This shook Seth awake and he manged to get his shoes on and get out just in time. He ran back towards the family home, and as he looked back, his summer house had flown thirty feet across the garden and into the swimming pool.

The storm hadn't broken us but as we sat and slurped our soup, we had a proper and frank discussion about the witches and the effects of the storm. We assumed that it was their plan to take down the South of England in full. There was no way they could have kept it quiet this time, but they could still have returned to kill us all and take everything for their own. In fact, they still could. We were worried that they may try something else and beat us when we were at our weakest. We planned to stay quiet until we had heard from Phil Lomas. Hopefully he could confirm that the diaries and letters were fake. We hadn't seen Phil at the meeting, so we needed to track him down over the next few days.

Saturday October 17th

The village was completely cut off from the rest of civilisation. The collapsed trees had entirely sealed off the main roads in and out of both ends of Danehill. We could already see people starting out to clear the debris and chop the broken trees. It was paramount that these routes were made open again, as none of the emergency services could get through if they were required. It was made clear to us that the school bus wouldn't be able to get through, and it would be a while before we were in the lessons again. This was something that gave us boys a rare glimmer of light in these dark days. What had been a ten-minute walk to get somewhere was now taking up to an hour, and every route we took was hazardous, and sometimes dangerous. There were branches and electricity cables still hanging precariously over houses, gardens and roads.

We were still without power, and communication was hard, but we were still getting snippets of stories about the storm and the aftermath. Every so often people would get a few minutes of radio signal and pass on their news. For instance, a ship had capsized at Dover, and a channel ferry had been driven ashore near Newhaven. The number of trees lost in the county of Sussex alone was apparently well over fifteen million. Sevenoaks in Kent was now being rather cruelly labelled as Two Oaks. Nobody had heard from Phil Lomas since the storm had erupted so the five of us decided to go and find him. We desperately needed to talk with him. We felt that he was the only person that could help our cause.

Sunday October 18th

The five of us met up near the church at nine o'clock. Pat had bought an axe to help us chop our way through any unwanted barriers we may have come across. Rabbit bought along a flask of tea. It was usually a casual ten-minute stroll to his house but today was going to take us much longer. There weren't many people about at that time in the morning. It was a nice day for a change, the sun was bright and there was a cool breeze in the air. We could hear the birds tweeting above us. Many of them had lost their homes in the storm. It was not as much as a struggle to get to the country lane as we thought. But when we were on the lane it began to get harder and harder. There were many trees crisscrossing over the road. It became clear that the reason nobody had seen Phil was because he had been isolated by the hurricane. A man his age could not have got out of there. I remember thinking that he must have been so scared and confused, I hoped that he had enough supplies. We had to get to him.

Eventually we made it to his house. It was hard to see the garden as it was now. When we had visited before we had all commented on how good it looked, how much care he took over his gardening. Now it just looked so sorry. The flowers looked as though they'd been dug over, but it was the power of the storm that had literally lifted them from their beds. They were shaded by broken down branches from the trees above. The flowers themselves were all dead and two trees had fallen in on his small summer house. Seth nudged me. My eyes followed his glance as he looked up to the sky. Phil's roof had caved in. The other lads had also noticed. This did not look good. We called out his name but could hear nothing in return. This did not look good at all.

We had to get in, and fast. Carter and Rabbit were already making their way down the now ravaged garden path to get to the front door. They furiously rapped on the front door calling out his name yet again. Pat then arrived on the scene. Without hesitation he screamed "GET OUT OF THE WAY". And took a huge swipe with the axe. The wooden door stood firm. But after a few more blows it cracked and weakened. He managed to squeeze himself through a gap and get inside. We all followed close behind. We ran up the stairs of the tiny cottage and swung open the door of one of the upstairs rooms of the two up two down property. The scene that greeted us was shocking.

I had never seen a dead body before. His eyes looked empty, and his lips were blue. His skin had turned pale and there was the faint rancid odour of death. It was obvious that he had been killed by the fallen roof. He was surrounded by rubble, and it was just his head and torso that we could see above the ruins. I had tears in my eyes, as did the others. It was a horrific scene. The sheer force of the hurricane had pushed the legs of his bed through the ceiling of the kitchen below.

It was an incredibly sad moment. We had only been here around three weeks before. We had shared a cup of tea and some biscuits with Phil at a table in his study. And now he was dead. However, there was one thing we had to do, and that was find the diaries. It felt disrespectful, rummaging through Phil's private things whilst his lifeless body laid still and alone upstairs, but we felt that Phil would want us to do this. If the manuscripts weren't fake, then Phil would want us to save the village he loved and respected so much. We trawled the whole of the small house, looking everywhere. After a couple of hours, we stopped and gave up. It was almost impossible. The papers might well have already been in the hands of the experts who Phil had said he'd wanted to view them. Or they could have been beneath the rubble upstairs. Either way, we weren't going to be finding them today. On the upside, we could keep it all quiet and not concern the other inhabitants of Danehill. We alerted one of the neighbours to his sad demise. She managed to send out word to the village doctor, as no ambulances could get through yet. Three hours later Lesley Turnbull turned up, and checked the body, to certify the death. He said that, amazingly, there was not one broken bone in his body. He had been suffocated by the rubble. It was hard to hear, and we left the little cottage broken men.

There had been so many instances over the past few months that had seen us grow as the men we would eventually become. Some of the things we'd seen or done had been enough to fill a lifetime for some, let alone a couple of months. We took the slow walk home, heads bowed, trudging over the trees, and between the debris strewn around the streets of our now unrecognisable village. Not a word was spoken between us. I doubted whether my life would ever be the same again after this. When I got home, I hugged my whole family hard. They too had heard the news. They praised me and the boys for finding Phil Lomas and helping the doctor. We also hoped that there weren't any other village people isolated and alone in their homes. The main thing now was for everyone to be there for others. It was all about the people, their lives and their futures. A devastation of horrific magnitude had occurred, and luckily, for now, people's coping mechanism had switched on, but they were still in shock. Once reality crept up on them then the aftermath would have more even far-reaching consequences.

Monday October 19th

The village were out in force on the Monday morning. There was no way that they could wait for help to arrive from the government and the authorities. These trees needed moving so that people could get out of the district, and supplies could be bought in. There were huge tree trunks strewn across the main roads roughly every quarter of a mile. There was no way that this was going to be a quick job, but it was urgent. Any person with a chain saw or an axe was called upon to assist. It took a huge group effort and was typical of the people of Danehill. There was a massive group, mainly men, that included my dad and his brother. They were working, slowly moving up the road, cutting the fallen trees and branches as they went. There was debris to clear, and many stops along the way, for health and safety reasons. It was a strenuous and demanding role, but they were all determined to pitch in. There were locals who needed medical attention and supplies, so stopping was not an option. The men split into two groups, so that one bunch of workers could rest whilst the others continued. It was chain gang of sorts and was working well.

My dad, my Uncle Peter and Ronny Braker's father Roy were on their break. They moved away from the constant droning of the chain saws and took a seat on a large, upturned branch just back from the main road. They opened their flask of tea and unwrapped their sandwiches ready for a well-earned respite. This experience was probably harder for them than most. They had grown up here and had lived in the village for over forty years. It was all they had known, and it now looked like a scene from a disaster movie. But they couldn't allow themselves to get sentimental. There would be plenty of time later for that. Now it was all about saving the lives of their friends and neighbours.

Something caught dads' eye as he looked out over the woodland before him. He was distracted, by a large bird flying past, almost knocking his food out of his hand. It was a crow, but the bird ignored his food. He had another meal lined up. It swooped down about thirty metres past where they were sitting and settled on a large rock. Dad could see the crow starting to peck at and pull on something sticking out of the ground. "What is that pesky bird chewing on?" said Roy. They strained their eyes to look a little closer. "It looks like…." Peter paused. "GET THE OTHERS." He shouted as he jumped up and began to run down to where the bird had perched.

Nigel Swanson arrived onsite an hour later. He was overseeing the area now. What dad had seen was a human forearm. He'd shooed the bird off and ushered the other twelve men working on the trees to get down there. The scene was that of utter desolation. It was a mass grave. It had been turned inside out by fallen trees during the storm. The huge roots of the great oak trees had ripped the soil apart, and there were now ten bodies visible to the naked eye. Nigel was taking notes about what they had found. He knew this wasn't down to the villagers, but everything had to be done officially. No other police forces could enter the parish at the current time, so he had to officiate alone over all that was going on. It was tough on Nigel, but he had the support of the whole village. He was having to cope with a whole new process, and something that he nor anyone else in the village had experienced before. He was used to dealing with petty thieves and poachers but now he had what might have been a mass slaughter on his hands.

The dead in the grave were not what anyone would have expected. If it wasn't peculiar enough as it was, there was also some other very distinct characteristics surrounding the dead. Their bodies were massive, and muscly and they were all around eight feet tall, and they were dressed in clothes reminiscent of Victorian times, and they were all perfectly restored, like they had all been in some sort of deep sleep, a type of hibernation, but they were dead. It was nightfall by the time everything had been sorted out at the grave. The road clearance would have to wait for another time. Hopefully the men at the other end of the village had manage to break through to get another route out and into the parish. Nothing could be done at this end until a proper investigation had been considered. It was a blow to morale.

When Dad arrived home, he explained to us all what had happened. He seemed in shock, and I didn't blame him. I felt the same after finding Phil Lomas, but this was different. There were ten bodies, and probably a much bigger story beneath their demise. I couldn't help thinking that I knew something about what had happened and who the dead were. I imagined that maybe this was good news, if this was the witches that we'd read so much about then maybe their reign of terror was over, and it was going to be a much happier ending after all.

Tuesday October 20th

The next day I caught up with the other boys. They'd heard the news and had the same thoughts as me. It was obvious that the dead were these evil witches from back in time. They had been killed by the power of the storm that they themselves had created. We were in the clear now. We planned to take some of our cash and use it to help rebuild the village. There was donation jars dotted around in several places throughout the area, so we could make a series of large cash injections to them without anybody getting suspicious or asking questions. We spent the afternoon climbing our way over and under wreckages to find the jars and manage to distribute around £40,000 to the cause.

In the evening, we made our way to the village hall for our nightly meal. More than thirty people from the district have been busy preparing food for everybody. The generator was still running well, and these evenings were a Godsend, especially for the elderly and the villagers who lived alone. It always turned into a carnival atmosphere after we'd all eaten. Tonight was even better. Everybody was happy because some mystery benefactors had donated huge amounts of monies to the cause of the village rebuild. Of course, Robin Hood was the talk of the village yet again. The five of us gave each other a wink. We had assisted our friends and neighbours yet again and were happy to stay out of the limelight. When we saw people taking to the stage to perform and provide entertainment for all, we were worried that the stage might fall in, but luckily, there was only a few people at a time who took centre stage. Some people sang, others told jokes and did terrible impressions. The Women's Institute put on plays and the historical society did talks, but these were always done with a tinge of regret; regret that Phil Lomas couldn't be there to share his wisdom and knowledge of the past from the village archives.

We were sitting at the back by the time that Mickey Hamble got on the stage and began to sing one of his old Irish folk songs. He had had a few too many whiskeys but nobody seemed to mind, and we all sang along with Hamble as he tried to entertain the masses in his own inimitable way. That was when the large village hall door creaked open loudly, and Giles Smedley entered the room. It was the first time we had seen him since the hurricane took hold of the village on that fateful night on the 16th of October. Giles looked tired. He looked emotional, and he looked sad. As he went to sit down next to us, he collapsed onto a chair fell to the floor with a loud thud. He lost consciousness and didn't come around for another hour.

When Giles eventually came round, he tried to explain what has happened on the night of the hurricane. There were a few of us stood round and we gave him as much space and air as possible to let him speak. But he was struggling to get his words out "I couldn't get to them. I tried so hard" he started to whimper, tears rolling down his cheeks. He was gasping for air, and by the time he started speaking again he wasn't making any sense. Lesley Turnbull stepped in and tried to calm him down. The doctor gave him a sedative. Giles was not in a state for anything.

It was dark, but the road was a bit clearer now, so a group of men were sent up to Chelwood Forest to check on the rest of the Smedley family. His mum and dad and sister had also not been present at the hall over the last few days. People had assumed they were away. The father was an airline pilot and was often out of the country. There was hope that maybe he was on holiday with his family. The fact that Giles was here now worried all of us. And when the group returned at 11 o'clock we could see from their faces that something was amiss, and something horrible had happened. The village hall was soon cleared save for Lesley Turnbull, Nigel Swanson and the vicar, David Kendall.

Wednesday October 21st

When I arrived at the village hall for breakfast the next day Giles was still there. I approached him to check if he was okay. It was obvious that he had spent the night at the hall. He still looked sleep starved, and his body looked very thin, as though he hadn't eaten for days. "Are you okay mate?" I asked. Giles murmured something about wanting to be left alone, and then realised it was me. He sat bolt upright and seemed more alive, it was as though I'd bought something out of him, whatever it was, I was just glad that he seemed to be getting better. Giles began to tell me what had occurred. It turned out that the family home had been badly hit during the hurricane. The chimney had been damaged and crashed through the roof of the house. It had killed both of his parents and his sister instantly. I ask Giles how he had survived the incident. He was incoherent by now, but I heard him say "I wasn't there".

In total thirty-four people were killed in the great storm of 1987, four of them sadly in our village alone. It was an awful loss of life, and I felt for Giles. Losing his whole family like this must have been dreadful. I couldn't comprehend it. Especially the fact that he had found their limp lifeless bodies with their lives taken out of them in such a horrible fashion. One thing I couldn't get my head around was the fact that he'd said he wasn't there. Why would anybody be out whilst the hurricane was blowing? Maybe he was still in a state of flux when I spoke to him, and he didn't know what he was saying. This had hit poor Giles hard. We were going to have to keep an eye on him, that was certain.

David Kendall had done the right thing and asked Giles to stay with him and his wife at the vicarage. The Smedley home was not the place Giles needed to be at this current time. They would have to wait for the outside World to be able to get back into the area to tend to his home and take care of his family within. But Giles didn't seem keen. He pleaded to be taken back to his house, and in the end the vicar succumbed, thinking that it was just something that Giles needed to get out of his system. There were more than enough locals to keep an eye, and pop into see Giles and aid his recovery. It was to be arranged that the bodies of the dead be moved to some freezers on a local dairy company's land on Fanyard Lane.

As I took a seat in the hall and started to eat my eggs and bacon, I saw Sir Harry Johnstone come in. The former Prime Minister was surrounded by his entourage. You wouldn't know that there had been all these horrible happenings in the village if you were judging it on him and his demeanour. He was doing the things that politicians always do when they know they need your votes; circling the room, checking if people were okay, offering support and aide to anybody that would listen. He was all smiles, waves and laughter, and people were still offering thanks for all that he had apparently done under the guise of the modern-day Robin Hood. He caught me looking and sauntered over. He knew not to play the politician with me by now. Eventually he walked over, sat down next to me and proceeded to talk.

Johnstone reminded me of his plans to host a party for the girl who had successfully had her brain tumour removed. He said that the parishioners needed this now more than ever. He had decided to throw a bash on the following Saturday evening. The girl (Daisy) was now back on terra firma and doing well. Her family had said that it was a fine idea and backed his notion. He said that he valued our input and advice, that we had been good to him, and felt that we too needed to be rewarded for our services to Danehill. I wasn't sure but told him we'd most probably all be there. He then stood up, cleared his throat, and raised his voice so that everybody in the village hall could hear him.

"Ladies and gentlemen, I am sorry to interrupt your delicious breakfast that has been beautifully prepared and served for you by these fine people. But the reason I am here today is because of villagers like these. They are the people who should be rewarded for the work they are doing during these testing times. I am sure you now, all know about Daisy, the poor young girl who had to visit the United States of America to have her brain tumour removed. I can report to you all today that she came home two nights before the storm, and she is doing well and in fine spirits. Luckily for them, I had put them up in one of my small holdings, so they were safe from the storm that came down upon us just a few nights back." He stopped to take in the applause and cheering before continuing with his well-rehearsed speech. "I would like to invite all and sundry to a party on the Larch Grove estate this Saturday at 8pm. It will be perfect time to celebrate her good health, and, also to say thank you to you; the good people of Danehill for all they have done over the last few days. I hope to see you all there. It will be an extravagant evening, laid on by me, with no expense spared, to offer you my thanks and support. Please do all spread the word to your fellow friends and family. I shall see you all on Saturday evening." He left the village hall to return to his mansion.

Later that day the five of us met up as usual. I told them of Sir Harry's plans. "I'm not sure" Rabbit commented, "Why does he need us. I get the fact that he feels bad, but to make some big show of thanking us. I'm pretty sure it will still be to his benefit. Maybe we should just come clean and admit everything." Carter butted in "No way. There's no need mate. And we've still got cash investments even after all our spending. We can still enjoy our money. The witches are dead, it's all over. Sod the investments. Once this is all over, I vote we get all of it back and spend it. We can travel the World." "That's all very well" I said "But how do we persuade our families that we just happened to find one million pounds? Because that's what we've still got left." Pat, Rabbit and Seth agree. "It's four to one Carter, let's just see for now. Let's see what happens at the party. You never know, maybe he'll do something decent for a change."

Friday October 23rd

The village clear up continued over the next couple of days. People worked extremely hard and Danehill was starting to look a little bit like we were used to. There was still much to do but we'd made a decent start. Giles Smedley was getting well looked after and joined the locals at the memorial hall on a nightly basis. There had been efforts to sort out his living accommodation, but the house was in an awful state. He still insisted on staying there though, so the best was made of the situation. Once he'd got over the shock, we were sure that he'd change his mind.

Saturday October 24th

We all gathered at the village hall on the Saturday evening. I met up with the boys outside. Johnstone had put his staff to work, and they been busy helping to clear the roads. But this wasn't to aid the village at all. He just did it to ensure that vehicles could drive from the village to his home, in preparation of getting everybody to his mansion for the party. He had laid on two or three minibuses. They would go back and forth from the hall to the Larch Grove Estate shuttling all of us guests. People felt that this impromptu party was actually a good idea. They could let their hair down and enjoy themselves after a horrible few days of village life. The chainsaw and axe gang could put down their tools, and the chefs could switch off their fires for the evening.

The minibus dropped us off at the gates of the estate. It was a long way down to the mansion, but we knew why Harry needed us to get out here. We were to get into golf carts at this point and make our way down the long winding drive. The estate had been turned into a political party broadcast. There were posters and banners everywhere praising the good work done by Sir Harry Johnstone. In the distance we could see fireworks going off into the dark nights sky. They lit up the horizon with the words 'Sir Harry for government" There were television cameras filming it all. We were all on film, no doubt being described as Johnstone voters. There were many of us. This is just what Harry wanted. It was so tacky and deplorable but very few people seemed to get what was going on; We were pawns in the Sir Harry Johnstone show, and he was putting on the performance of a lifetime. The house looked like it had been restored to its former glories. There had been no expense spared and it looked like a different property to the one we had been to before.

It was ridiculous. There was no mention at all about Daisy and her family. It was all about him. We could see nothing that praised the village or us for that matter. Once inside we were greeted by smartly dressed servers with plates mounted with canapes, and flutes of champagne. There were press in the great hall, rapidly scribbling down notes in their pads, there were TV reporters doing pieces to camera, and in the corner, hidden away were Daisy and her family. We went over to say hello and check on her wellbeing.

It was great to see her looking so well. I have to say I felt so proud that we had been instrumental in making this happen. We all felt a warm glow inside. The death of Phil Lomas, and the Smedley Family, as well as the trauma that Daisy had to go through certainly put life into perspective. Johnstone saw us all and saluted, but he looked a little awkward when we ignored him. He was still wary of us and was right to be so. We had had a big hand in where he now was after all.

The soiree went long into the night. Johnstone had pulled out all the stops. He wanted the whole of the United Kingdom to see. Why else would he have invited the media. This wasn't about the village or the community, or even about Daisy; this was all about him. You could sense the locals were getting restless. They had come to see Daisy, and how she was. Her family were well known and liked around Danehill. Some people just couldn't see through the façade that Harry was putting on, but they just wanted to give the poor girl their best wishes, and then retire to bed. It had been a hard few days and weeks for everyone. Sir Harry Johnstone then stood up in front of his guests.

"Thank you all for coming to my party". He started, "This is a huge celebration of the people of this village. I want to thank you all for our tireless good work you have done in rebuilding the village and the sense of wellbeing since the storm. I'd like to thank the five lads who found the unfortunate Chairman of the Historical Society (He didn't even know Phil's name). I would also like you all to raise a glass to Daisy and her family. She is now doing well and is on the mend since her successful operation. I paid for the most successful surgeons stateside to handle her care in America, and they did a fine job. Please can you all raise a glass to Daisy. Cheers to her and her family." Everybody got to their feet and raised their flutes of champagne and clapped Daisy as she took to the stage. It looked as though she was keen to speak, but she was ushered off the stage before she could open her mouth.

The rest of the speech was all about Sir Harry and his hopes and dreams for future. It was all for the cameras. He stated that he would be donating a huge amount of his funds in helping rebuild parts of the village that the storm has decimated. The rest of this oration was all about the supposed marvellous exploits of the Conservative party, and how great Thatcher was. He made several disparaging remarks about the Labour party, and then continued to praise himself, and tell everybody about all the good work he has in mind for the future good of the country. A few of the villagers now started to leave the party. They could now see this for what it was. They began to slope off as Johnstone was still on the stage. He could see them leaving, but there was nothing he could do. The press also noticed, and the television cameras quickly whipped around to catch them all leaving on film. This was embarrassing for Johnstone but there was not a lot he could do. I don't think the fact that some people leaving would have stopped him getting back into government, but it would surely put a dent in his plans, and his ego would suffer.

We stayed right until the bitter end. We had decided beforehand that we were going to make the most of the free food and drink. Sir Harry had been ushered off quite quickly after his speech, and we saw no more of him for the rest of the night. The party continued for about fifty of the villagers that had stayed with us to ensure they had drunk Harry dry. Some were dancing to the band, whilst others were having fun snooping around the great house. It was good to see Giles Smedley there and Rabbit and I went over to see how he was. He didn't look too upset for a guy that had just lost his family in the way that he had. In fact, Giles looked more annoyed than anything. "I hope the five of you are free tomorrow afternoon." He said "I think it would be in your best interests to meet with me. I know exactly what you have been up to." I looked at Rabbit, he looked back at me. "I'm not sure what you are talking about Giles but okay, no problem" I said, it was all I could muster, especially after a night of drinking free alcohol, and we walked off to grab the other three boys and made our way home back to the village. What was to come tomorrow was anybody's guess.

Sunday October 25th

The five of us met up by the village hall on the Sunday morning. It was still busy there. Most of the electricity and phone lines were now back on in the village but the hall had now become a real hub. Villagers were still gathering onsite to have food, drink hot drinks, and chat. The elderly were especially grateful. The district had really come together since the storm, and it was great that this was continuing. We still had another week before we were to return to our studies, as the school, and the college, were not yet up and running properly. It was a nice day, and we sat on the swings in the children's play area for a quick chat before we made the walk up to the now decaying Smedley house and our encounter with Giles.

I spoke first "He could be lying" Pat was not impressed either. "Let's face it, he could mean anything. He might just mean that he knows that we have been helping Johnstone" "I'm not sure" Rabbit said, "He had a knowing look in his eye. I think he's onto us." Carter agreed "I get that, but so what? There is nothing he can do about it. There's only one of him, and he's not exactly in a great state now. How is he going to prove anything? I think we turn up and hear him speak." We all agreed. We should hear what he had to say and decide on what we then do. There were five of us and just one of him. We could easily scare him if he threatened to let on what we'd been up to over the past few months, and we doubted he had any proof anyway. So, we all set off up the hill to Chelwood Forest and our meeting with Giles Smedley.

By the time we reached Giles' place it was noon. The top floor of the now battered house was exposed to the elements. The chimney breast had caved in, and you could see the imperilled bedroom furniture from the roadside. The locals had put up a façade of bed sheets, which were blowing in the October wind, but you could still clearly see the devastation behind them. We didn't understand why he would want to stay here. It was like a scene from a World War two film post blitz. But as your eyes took in the wider view of the detached homes either side, they were in perfect condition, it was as if the wind had purposely missed the properties to the left and right of the Smedley homestead. It was as though this was meant.

We had not seen Giles sitting downstairs in the front garden. He was lying back in an armchair, which had fallen from the destructed first floor room, which was clearly visible to any visitors. "You lads have been busy, haven't you?" he said, he looked like he had taken on a role as a Bond villain, minus the cat being stroked on his lap. He looked very different, as though the death of his family had given him a new strength. It was weird. He didn't look broken anymore; it was like his tragedy had never happened. He couldn't have been acting when we saw him in the hall, that day he looked broken, as if he would never get over the loss of those close to him. Now, though, his face, his expression, his idiom – it all seemed atypical. "You had me guessing for a while. I had my doubts whether you lot would be capable of this, but you've impressed me. You've impressed me with the way you have managed to keep this quiet from the rest of Danehill. You have impressed me by the way you've helped people. I'm disappointed but impressed." Seth was having none of this. "What are you talking about?" he asked. "Shut up Seth. Don't insult my intelligence. I know it was you five who stole my money. YOU BROKE INTO THE VILLAGE HALL AND STOLE ALL OF MY MONEY." He was angry now, and he was shaking whilst he shouted. "YOU TOOK MY ANTIQUES, YOU TOOK MY JEWELS, YOU TOOK MY FUTURE AWAY" He then hushed his voice to almost a whisper. "And now you will have to pay." This was getting decidedly weird "The only saving grace for you is that you didn't find it all. I think you need to know what has been going on."

"I have pieced it all together now. Do you all remember that night back in June? I saw you on the road on the tractor. We spoke. I knew you were up to no good, you wondered why I was out that late. But we said nothing to each other, the boys code; you keep quiet, and I'll keep quiet, fair enough. You could have been up to anything, so I kept that bit of information to myself. But it did get me thinking. I was expecting somebody else to be in that tractor, I didn't expect to see Ronny in the driving seat, that threw me for a bit, but I met my 'friends' further down the road." He mimed quotation marks as he said this. "You see, I was off to the hall that night to help myself to some of my cash. But where I got there it was all gone. THE WHOLE PLACE WAS EMPTY!" He rose his voice again. "ALL OF IT GONE. I should have followed you that night, maybe then things wouldn't have got this far. Maybe I could have retrieved my stuff. Maybe I wouldn't have had to have Eddie killed." This stopped us in our tracks. "Yes, that's right lads, Eddie is no more. Apparently, he took a fall down some very steep steps". Giles was laughing now. "You see, those friends of mine in the tractor are not what you would call people. Not in the conventional sense anyway." He used quotation marks again 'They are 'The Helpers'. And they are mine; they are under MY control. They paid a visit to Eddie last night. The poor old fella is very clumsy, especially on slippery steps. I hope the Helpers don't have to visit any of you in the future."

"I found it very bizarre when so many people in the village were suddenly in the money; mortgages paid off, holidays booked, and brain tumours sorted. People really like to gossip in Danehill. Everybody knows everybody else's business. I certainly know all about yours. That night at the disco; I overheard you chatting, you seemed as though you were up to no good. Something was definitely amiss. Once again, I should have realised. But then you threw a spanner in the works, didn't you? That old git Johnstone took all the plaudits. Now that certainly confused me. But why would he suddenly turn? Why would he suddenly become a concerned citizen? I saw you on the night that everybody got their gift's, but you were clever and wore balaclavas, I have been so close to catching you in the act so many times. You put on that party too – You boys have been so busy. I just needed that last little bit of proof to be sure that it was you. So, I went to see Poor old Eddie, the man who knows everything. Eddie and his dubious investments – I really didn't think that he'd keep a record of his dodgy dealings, but there it all was in black and white, all your names in his ledger. So, it's obvious to me now that you are the thieves, you are the people who robbed me, you are the lads who have stolen my birthright. And now you, and all the villagers, will have to pay. But first I'd like you all to know exactly what has been going on. I don't think you are going to like this story."

We were all absolutely stunned. Giles Smedley was apparently some sort of gangster Don! It sounded ludicrous, but maybe there was something in this. It could have been a fanciful tale but, after all that we had seen and done over the past few months, anything seemed possible. Giles had some explaining to do...

"Back in 1487 the village of Danehill was at war with the village of Worsted Haynes. 500 years ago, these two places did not get on at all. There were great lakes in Worsted Haynes, as there still are today, and they were full of fish. The locals of Danehill would fish there regularly, but the Worsted locals didn't like this. So, they waged war on their near neighbours. What the Danehill residents didn't know was that Worsted Haynes was governed by witches. They were not witches in the traditional sense, as they were both male and female. These witches had special powers and could bring terror and devastation to the World. The Danehill soldiers were winning the war with Worsted Haynes, and so the witches decided to bring it to an end. They created a huge typhoon, that cut through the village and killed every living soul. The Worsted Haynes witches then travelled to Danehill and took all the belongings of the dead. They still had their lakes, so they would always have plenty to eat. But now they were also very rich, and the village of Danehill was completely obliterated. The witches would then gain strength, and go into hibernation, they would then sleep for a century. They would leave a team of two hundred Helpers to guard the treasure whilst they rested. Around eighty years later the village of Danehill began to flourish once more. New people settled there and lived their lives like anybody else at that time. But the witches of Worsted Haynes came out of hibernation in 1587 and were jealous, and so they decided to kill all the inhabitants of Danehill once again."

Giles then went onto explain to us how, every hundred years, the process would begin again; the witches would wake from their deep sleeps and bring great destruction to Danehill, they would kill, pillage and plunder everything they could, and bring forth one last scene of desolation that would end it all for the villagers. They repeated this up until 1987. Each time getting stronger and each time getting richer. In fact, they got so rich that they couldn't spend all the money, hence the fact that they felt the need to safely bury their findings where nobody could find them; or so they thought. As the World gathered pace, and people started to grow, the witches realised they had to move with the times. They made the decision to come together and put all their powers into the hands of one family, and that family would be the benefactors of all their wrong doings. They would have the perfect little family, living a perfect little life, whilst being guardians of all the treasure and money. And, of course, they would have a merry band of Helpers to guard them and to keep an eye on their treasure."

"And they chose us; the Smedley's." Giles was enjoying this. "You see, we then have everything. We have all your belongings, all your money, all your history. But this time the plan was bigger. I made the decision to ruin the whole of the South of England. I deserve everything. This hurricane was meant to kill everyone from Cornwall to London." I butted in. "That didn't work this time though did it sunshine? Because your hurricane killed the witches whilst they slept. My Dad found their bodies. So, what happened? If they were asleep, how did the hurricane start?" "It's not just them that have the powers SUNSHINE" Giles replied. Who else do you think could have done all of this?" "It didn't work though Giles. Humans are more resolute in the twentieth century. It takes a lot to bring us down. We're not in the dark ages anymore."

"I'll be honest" Giles responded. "I underestimated humanity, and I certainly underestimated you lot! The spoils are always well guarded by the Helpers but if there was one weekend when I thought they could be helping me in other ways it was the Centenary Weekend. That Saturday night the Helpers were stationed across the whole of the South of England working to start this hurricane; the hurricane that was meant to end all hurricanes. And then you five decided to rob me. You were very lucky. You would have been killed if they were there that night. The facts are that, yes, you are right, the witches are all dead. But I am still here, and I have all the power. I still have many riches too – you won't ever find them."

We had so many questions. And Giles had all the answers. It surprised us that he was happy to give us all this information. We now would have all the knowledge to go to the authorities and bring Giles Smedley down once and for all. Carter was first to ask "Excuse my French Smedley, but this does sound like a load of old bollocks to me. If this, and all these old diaries and manuscripts are all true then why are there never any bodies? If people move in and the village is rebuilt, then surely there would be mass graves everywhere. You can't kill a couple of thousand people and get rid of that many bodies." "Oh Carter" said Giles, "How do you think they stay so powerful? Why do you think the witches need to hibernate for so long? In fact, what do bears do before they go into hibernation – they eat – A LOT. "That's rank" Pat said. "So, they eat the dead? You are full of shit Giles." "The thing is Pat, those bodies that Sams dad found aren't here anymore. Because I ate them. You can go and check with the local copper. He won't find them. The police tape is still there, and so are the skeletons but that's it. I am now stronger than any of those witches that came before me.

I have all their power now. I am more powerful than they ever were."

"That is disgusting Giles. And I've got a question" Rabbit said. "Where are the Helpers now then?" "If you think I'm telling you that Rabbit, then you've got another thing coming." Giles laughed again. "I can't give away all my secrets." There was something very sinister about all this. Giles was right, why should he tell us all of this? The power had gone to his head. This was an even more worrying situation than he had already explained. He was power hungry and didn't care who knew. Unhinged? Maybe. Disturbed? Definitely. Irrational? Yes. Deranged? I would not have been surprised. This wasn't going to end well for anyone, least of all, us. We had taken most of his treasure. The storm though had taken his family, and this only added to his strange demeanour. Rabbit continued to grill him, "If the Smedley family are so strong and the rest of us are so weak, then how did the hurricane kill the rest of your family so easily?" "The storm didn't kill them Rabbit, I did.

They were not really my family not in the normal sense, not to me, they might have bought me into the World, but they were weak. They weren't happy to be the chosen ones. I knew when we got word of the hurricane that they would warn all of you, and I had to stop them. They would have told the whole of the nation what was happening if they could have. I want all this power and riches to myself. The hurricane was the witches' idea but killing the family was mine. The witches agreed to it too. All I had to do was leave the house and let the hurricane do its thing. The witches don't like weak minded fools either. Well, they didn't until very recently. They obviously weren't as clever as they thought; letting a little bit of wind kill them like that whilst they slept. Very silly that." Rabbit wanted to know what was going to happen next. Giles was very calm with his answer, "I can't tell you that boys. Just know that it won't be good. You have done me so much wrong recently. You, and all the villagers will have to be punished, and it's all your fault. You couldn't leave well alone, could you? You should have just left my treasures underneath the village hall. You see, if you had done that, then the hurricane would still have killed the witches, but I would still have all that I need. I could have left Danehill with all this power and riches and nobody would ever have known any of this, but now I just want revenge. It will come but you won't know when." "How do you know we won't leave here and tell the government and the army about this?" Pat said. "Because you have seen what I did to my family Pat. If you say anything to anybody about this then all your families will die a horrible death. I guarantee it. That is my promise to you." "But we've got friends in high places now" I said. Giles laughed, "Old Harry? Ha. I don't think he'll be helping you. I've got plans for that old bastard."

We left Giles and started the walk home back to the village. We were forlorn. And all trudged home at a slow pace. The scattered obstacles from the storm slowed us down but it was more than that. We felt battered and bruised, we felt lost, but most of all we felt beaten. The last few months had been a roller coaster of emotions; from the highs of the findings at the village hall, to the fun we had spending the money, from the thrill of helping others to the awful night of the hurricane, and now to this. We had all the knowledge, but we could do nothing with it. Our friends and families would be killed if we tried anything. We would just have to sit and wait; wait for Giles' next move.

Wednesday October 28th

Three days later we decided that we had to tell Sir Harry what had happened. We would go to his estate and ask for his help. He had to believe us. He knew half the story. He knew that we had found all the treasure. He was also well-aware of Eddie's involvement with us. If he now knew that Eddie was dead, then that would give us more ammunition to convince him with. Johnstone could then use the power that he now had returned to him, because of us, to sort out this mess. He could have Giles incarcerated at her majesty's pleasure, and maybe we could all move on with our lives. Maybe Giles was far too powerful for that now, but we had to try something. We took the long walk up to the Larch Grove Estate to confront Harry with our information. Maybe it was a long shot, but we had to give it a go. We reached the gates and were surprised to find them open. The intercom was broken, and there was no sign of any estate staff as we walked up the long driveway. It felt different to the last time we were here. That night there was an atmosphere in the air. There was a certain confidence to the place. It was over the top and all geared towards Harry, but it was there.

Now it was eerily quiet. You could have heard a pin drop as we approached the large house that Johnstone called home. We reached the large front door and went to knock but the door was already open and made a loud creaking sound as Pat pushed it to reveal the massive entrance hall inside. We called out his name but got no answer. Suddenly, a large raven cawed loudly, and we all jumped out of our skins as it flew past us, brushing its wings against my face as it escaped to the outside. We yelled for Harry once more but got no response once again. Something caught our eager eyes, and we all looked up at the high ceiling above us and that is when we saw Sit Harry Johnstone the former Prime Minister of Great Britain.

The body was swinging gently about thirty feet above us. The strength of the thick rope tied tightly round his neck, and the other end, to the antique chandelier ensuring it didn't fall. The great hall of the Johnstone family home, that had looked so resplendent on the night of the party was now a cold unwelcoming place, and a shadow of its itself. We couldn't get the body down it was too high. We rang Nigel Swanson, who was in turn contacted the coroner, so we sat and waited for them to arrive. It looked like Sir Harry had committed suicide, but it would have been a struggle to have got himself up that high onto the beams without anybody's help. There seemed to be something more sinister at play.

The fact that the estates staff were also non-existent made it even stranger. We found the number of the head butler and rang him.

He said that he'd had word from Sir Harry and had been told to take a couple of days of leave along with the rest of the workforce. Rabbit and Seth had been sitting in the kitchen and came out to see us in the hall a few minutes later "I found this on the worktop." said Rabbit. It was a note, and it was addressed to us.

'Did you really think I'd let him help you? Did you really think I'd let it go? Did you really think I'd let him live? Did you really think that he'd be able to help you? Do you still think you will survive this?

I would keep this quiet if I were you. We don't want anyone else coming to harm. I think it's best that you burn this note now. Go home and spend a bit of precious time with your families, you might not get much more time together.

Kind regards,

Your friendly neighbourhood 'Helper'

It was clear that Smedley had killed him. He was playing games with us now. We didn't know but this seemed to be the beginning of something rather than the end. We'd seen what he was capable of after the death of his parents and sister. And now he had managed to get to someone before we could. He was a step ahead of us every time. He'd taken this battle and was winning the war. The press would have a field day with the death of Johnstone. This wouldn't help Smedley as the media of the World would be converging on the village as soon as the news was out. We judged that this meant something was going to happen very soon. His plan for the locals was certainly now all apparent. We felt that we should stay and wait for Nigel, but the note had spooked us. We decided to leave and walk back to the village.

It was now gone five o'clock. It was dark and it was cold. The roads were now mostly cleared of the storm debris, but we still preferred to walk down the main road back to the village, and our homes. Like the walk back from the Smedley's just three days before; we were solemn and quiet. It wasn't just us that were quiet, the early Autumn sunset meant that the birds had stopped chirping, and all we could hear as we walked down the A275 main road was the sound of the rustling of branches and leaves blowing in the wind. Everything was now back up and running so we spotted a few kitchen and sitting room lights aglow in the distance. It was comforting to us that people were getting back to their normal lives since the hurricane. Little did they know though was that something else could be on the way that might, once again interfere with their day to day living. We talked a bit, mainly about Giles and Johnstone. It was frightening to think that Smedley was now some sort of evil demon. As we started out on the final piece of the journey past Cobnor House we could hear a distant rumbling. It sounded like the engine of a Jumbo Jet. It got closer and closer and louder and louder. It got so loud that we couldn't hear each other as we shouted in concern at what was happening. We were shaking, and it felt as though the area beneath our feet was moving. And then it just stopped as quickly as it had started, as though nothing had occurred. We looked across the road at the school. There were sights and sounds of static crackling and fizzing on the telephone lines above our heads, like lightning, and then an excessively loud bang that almost burst our ear drums, and everything went silent again. The lights of the school buildings went out and then I heard the loudest sound I have ever heard in my life. It was a massive crack. Then silence again. None of us had a clue about what was going on.

We decided to run, and run we did. All five of us just had to get back home to our families. We were so worried. Giles Smedley was a massive worry in our lives now, and it was clear that he had done something. As we ran the last two miles into the village and down towards the village hall, we could see that the light in there was the only one that could be seen for a long way around. It was lucky that the generator was still on. Straightaway we recognised our loved ones they were all part of a large throng that all gathered inside and outside the hall in the centre of Danehill. People had been quick to gather there ever since the storm of twelve days before, it was a safety net for all and sundry. People were confused, they had all heard the ridiculously loud noise and nobody could figure out what had been going on.

Nigel Swanson was stood at the front of the hall on the stage with a loud-speaker and spoke to the crowd that had summoned before him. "Ladies and gentlemen of Danehill. This is a very difficult thing for me to say to you all, especially since the hurricane but I must address you and let you know that another disaster has occurred that is, once more, endangering our lives. I have just got off the phone with the Sussex chief of Police in Brighton. He has informed me that an earthquake on the Richter scale of 10.7 has hit Danehill. It is the highest ever recorded in the history of man." Once again, our community was cut off from the rest of the World.

People were very scared. There was wailing and crying bellowing from the audience. Nigel continued "But I need to tell you all that there is some light at the end of the tunnel. Apparently, the earthquake happened in a perfect circle, which has meant that, although the village has been affected and we are now all actually living on an island." This was very strange. There were now two police helicopters circling above us. The lights from the aircraft were pointing down on us lighting everybody up in the car park of the village hall. Suddenly the wind picked up, and both the helicopters started to shake. It was as though a big hunting dog had taken them in his jaws like a startled rabbit and was tossing them side to side. The wind was getting stronger and stronger. "CAN EVERYBODY PLEASE MOVE DOWN TO THE FRONT SO THAT WE CAN GET EVERYONE ELSE INSIDE THE HALL TO SAFETY."

Nigel continued to try and put everyone at ease, but it wasn't working. There were still many people outside, caught in the elements, transfixed on what was going on above them in the night skies. Then just like it had done outside the school, everything went silent. There was another massive crack, and both helicopters started hurtling towards the ground. Within thirty seconds they had both hit the recreation ground at break-neck speed and burst into flames. A whole crowd of villagers ran down towards the wreckage but there was no way that anybody would have survived the accident. Nigel then joined the throngs of crowd outside and started to organise and coordinate them all. People with fire extinguishers were running down to try and put the fire out.

There was no way any ambulances could enter the village now, being as though we were effectively surrounded by a canyon. Whilst people were trying desperately to extinguish the fires, Nigel addressed us all again. He had to shout over the panicked voices "LADIES AND GENTLEMEN. PLEASE STAND BACK. PLEASE RETURN TO YOUR HOMES. THIS IS TOO DANGEROUS. THE FIRE WILL NOT SPREAD, THERE IS NOTHING YOU CAN DO. IT IS TOO

BIG A FIRE TO PUT OUT. WE WILL MEET AGAIN IN THE MORNING TO DISCUSS WHAT ARE PLANS WILL BE. I WILL GET IN CONTACT WITH THE CHIEF ONCE AGAIN. PLEASE TRY NOT TO WORRY. ALL WILL BE OKAY. BY THE MORNING THE FIRES WILL BE EXTINGUISHED. LET'S RECONVENE HERE AGAIN AT 9AM TOMORROW."

We all left and headed for home. Mum and Dad, Nan, and me and Sasha all sat in the front room. Once again, we were surrounded by petrified pets. We were chatting away, trying to keep cheerful. I didn't want to say anything about Giles Smedley and the death of Johnstone. There was enough going on without worrying my family even more. They had enough to contend with now. We sat and told familiar family tales and made each other laugh with memories of our past. It turned into an evening of reminiscing. It was the first time in a while when everybody let go and allowed themselves to be silly.

Then the rain started. It was pitiful at first. Just a light drizzle, with the pitter patter of rain drops tapping against the windows. But within the space of a couple of minutes it got harder and harder and louder and louder. It must have rained hard for about one and a half hours. The sound was like stones hitting the floor and vibrating up to hit the windows. It was so powerful that it rebounded off the garden and hit the windows of our bedrooms on the first floor of the house, almost fifteen feet above. My family felt safe in this environment, sipping away on their cups of cocoa. To them this was just a heavy rainstorm, but I sat there and prayed under my breath. I was ninety-nine percent sure that Smedley was behind all of this. It was a downpour of biblical proportions, and it shook the village to its very core. And then suddenly it went silent. No rain, no wind and no earthquakes, just calm. Was it all over? It appeared to be. We sat up for a couple of hours more, and then retired to bed, leaving the rabbits and guinea pigs to sleep in safely padded cardboard boxes.

Thursday October 29th

The following morning, we took the short walk to the village hall. Nigel Swanson was already there, dressed smartly in a fluorescent jacket, and equipped with a torch, some rope, and a first aid kit. He had heard from the chief of Sussex police via walkie talkie, and it was not good news. Apparently, the Worsted Lakes had overflowed due to the severe flooding the previous night. This was astonishing as the rainfall had lasted for just about two hours. It must have been one of the strongest and strangest rainfalls ever. Once again, my thoughts turned to Giles Smedley, but I had to put that to the back of my mind. I really wanted to mention something to Officer Swanson, but I couldn't do a thing without discussing it with the other four lads first. We found some seats in the hall and waited. People around us looked nervous, others scared, and some even excited. Nigel held the loudspeaker to his mouth once more.

"VILLAGERS OF DANEHILL, MY FRIENDS AND NEIGHBOURS. I AM SAD TO SAY THAT I BRING YOU BAD NEWS ONCE MORE. THE POLICE OFFICERS INVOLVED IN THE HELICOPTER CRASH LAST NIGHT HAVE SADLY PERISHED. AND I WOULD LIKE TO HOLD A MINUTE'S SILENCE TO HONOUR THEIR DEATHS." Everybody bowed their heads and got lost in their own thoughts for the following sixty seconds. I was still thinking about Giles and what we should do. I imagined the others were doing the same. A minute later Nigel continued "THANK YOU EVERYBODY. I AM AFRAID THAT OUR VILLAGE HAS BEEN PUT IN A STATE OF NATIONAL EMERGENCY. THE RAIN-STORM LAST NIGHT HAS CAUSED A MASSIVE FLOOD, AND THE WORSTED HAYNES LAKES HAVE BURST THEIR BANKS. THE TONNES AND TONNES OF WATER FROM THE LAKES HAVE FILLED THE CANYON THAT SURROUNDED US. WE ARE SURROUNDED BY A RIVER THAT IS TEN MILES WIDE. NOW OBVIOUSLY THIS ISN'T GREAT NEWS BECAUSE WE ARE STILL AN ISLAND, BUT WHAT IT DOES MEAN IS THAT PEOPLE FROM THE OUTSIDE CAN BRING US FOOD AND

MEDICINES VIA BOAT. THERE IS NOT A LOT MORE THAT CAN BE DONE TODAY SAVE FOR WAITING ON SUPPLIES. I WILL TAKE A SMALL TEAM OUT TO INVESTIGATE BUT I WANT ALL AND SUNDRY TO RETIRE TO THEIR HOMES FOR NOW." Another get-together was called for the next day. I walked home with the family. I didn't see my mates that day. It felt right to spend the afternoon with my family. Once again, we enjoyed being cocooned in each other's company, we played board games, ate food, and chatted and laughed under candlelight. The way everything was working out, I wasn't sure how much more time I would get to spend with them, so every minute was precious.

It was that time the locals were spending with their loved ones which put a stop to people leaving for the outside World as soon as we had found out how perilous our lives had become. It was also the want of the villagers to help each other. Nigel Swanson had advised us all to stay at home and stay safe. The massive downpour had filled the cavernous area around Danehill, but it had also affected homes and landowners in the parish. So, instead of listening to Swanson that afternoon people were out and about aiding the afflicted. It was a massive team effort and as ever the Danehillians didn't disappoint. Sandbags were placed at the front of people's homes who were situated at the bottom of steep streets or valleys. The sandbags would offer protection to properties where water would flow freely to if more rain was to arrive. There was a real herculean effort to make the village a safer place. There was much concern that things were going to get worse before they got better, and neighbours and friends needed their minds putting at rest.

Several homes on the village outskirts had been flooded severely and these were the first people facilitated. A team of locals were sent out to get the families from their very wet homes and into accommodation with friends. It would take months to sort but once the houses had been sorted and dried, they would be able to return. The same thing couldn't be said of belongings, which had been ruined in the flood. Animals had to be rescued from fields that had been destroyed by the waters. People really stepped up to help the needy and the community spirit was coming to the fore once more. The number of locals who volunteered for their own properties to be used as temporary housing was huge, and people were back, and feeling more secure in the bosom of the village. Of course, it didn't help that we were only just getting over the furore of the hurricane. There was still much to be done in rebuilding people's lives from that, and now that the problems had become much worse, efforts to help had more than doubled. By the end of Thursday night, everyone seemed a lot happier; safe in the knowledge that everybody who needed help had received it in spades.

Friday October 30th

The locals were fretting. We were all stood inside the village hall. We had been waiting for Nigel Swanson for around an hour. His family were there but he wasn't. His wife, Joan, had said that Nigel informed her he was going to be following right behind her and the kids. Joan was concerned and so after a while, a few of the villagers walked up the road to the police house. The lads and I followed behind, fearing the worst. When we all arrived, three men entered and came out ten minutes later carrying the lifeless body of Nigel Swanson. They had found him at the bottom of the stairs. The consensus was that he had fallen down the stairs and broken his neck. It was a sad state, a sad state that the five of us were sadly now getting used to witnessing. We had now been at the discovery of three dead bodies in the space of just two weeks. At least we couldn't blame Giles Smedley for this death. Everybody quickly returned to the memorial hall, and let the family know what had happened. They were led away to the vicarage for prayers and consoling. Doctor Lesley Turnbull then took to the stage to address everybody and continue with the meeting. We now had no way of contacting the police as nobody could find the walkie talkie at the police house. Nigel was also the only person with the codes to enter the village CB radio frequency. It was decided that the only way we could get to help would be to find a boat to sail over the newly created river. But the only families who owned boats were rich people with sailing boats that were permanently moored at Brighton Marina and the reservoir nearby in the parish of Forestry Row. It was decided that we should keep searching in the hope that surely somebody somewhere could sort us out with a vessel or two.

Once again, the village of Danehill and its occupants, were on their own. This was going to take a lot of working out. At least the outside World were aware of our predicament so stuff could be either flown in or brought to us by boat. We would just have to wait – for now. Just as before, people tended to congregate in the centre of the village, and the village hall once again became the main hub for information and food. The generator was still running, and we had some food to keep us going. The local famers were generous with their crops, so we were not going to starve. For the next couple of days everybody came together. There were big football matches put on between lads and dads, a party was organised on the memorial green beneath the church, there was a barn dance, and somebody bought down an old piano to entertain the elderly with some old-time tunes. That sense of community had still not left us, and people soon forgot about the troubles and strife. It was fun. I spent a great amount of my time with my four friends. We were continuing to keep our information to ourselves. We still had almost one million pounds hidden away in investments, and we wanted to use this to help, if we could. But Eddie was now dead, and we had no way of getting hold of that cash. Locals were concerned that they had not seen or heard from Giles since the night of the rainstorm. We were worried too, but for very different reasons.

Sunday November 8th

It had been ten days now. Since the death of our local police man, we had had no contact at all from the outside World. No boat had been found, so there was no way in getting out to contact anybody. Several villagers had tried to swim the newly formed river that encircled us, but the current was just too strong to navigate.

The head of the Sussex police force had not been in touch, and no deliveries had been forthcoming. It was a worrying time. Nobody could understand why the provisions promised from the nearby towns were non-existent. I met with the boys, and we took a football onto the recreation ground for a game of headers and volleys. We purchased some beer from the local shop and spent the afternoon enjoying ourselves. It was as though we didn't have a care in the World but the whole Giles Smedley debacle, and the village now sitting in the middle of a vast expanse of water was always at the back of our minds. We finished playing at six o'clock and none of us wanted to go home so we decided to take a stroll through the woods up to the Wagon and Ponies. It was dark, and we didn't know the way. Just a couple of weeks back we could have done it with our eyes closed. But the storm had totally obliterated the woodland before us. The landscape had changed and there were fallen trees everywhere. Our usual route was out of the question, so we made do and tried the walk on instinct alone. What should have taken an hour was now into its third, and we were totally lost. Our eyes were now accustomed to the autumnal dusk, but we couldn't work out where we were. We heard a noise, a splash about fifty yards to our left, and went to investigate. There was a figure pulling something large, and as we approached, we saw that this shadowy character was pulling a boat from water. We had reached the edge of this newly formed island, on which Danehill, and all the Danehillians, now found themselves situated. There was a country lane right next to the river. We had managed to go about half a mile out of our way in our fruitless search for the pub. The person turned around. It was Giles Smedley.

"Oh, Hello boys" he said. Obviously startled at being seen. He'd certainly been caught in the act. He was carrying Nigel Swansons walkie talkie. "So, it was you that killed Nigel then" Seth said. He then launched himself at Giles, desperately trying to punch him, and bring him down. Pat reacted quickly and pulled Seth back. "Don't do it Seth. He's not worth it." Giles Smedley had us over a barrel, any sort of move on him by us would mean awful things happening to our families. Seth pulled clear of Pats grasp and landed a massive punch square on Giles' nose. He went down easily. Smedley stayed on the ground, wiping his now broken nose that was dripping blood. "I'm gonna give you that one Seth. But that's it, no more. I understand your frustration at this situation, emotions are high, but one more like that and you, and all your families, are going to be killed. He gained back his composure and stood up. Seth was still angry. He was usually a very chilled character but seeing Giles with the walkie talkie had clearly riled him. "Do you really think you're going to get away with this?" Pat was now joining in. "I already have Pat." Replied Giles. "You have got to calm down, all of you. This won't end well." 'How can it end well anyway? Rabbit asked. "How do we stop this? What is going to happen now? There must be a way we can come to some agreement to stop this façade." "Just stay quiet for now. I will tell you when it's over. If you play along, then all will be fine. I just need some time." He then went onto explain what he had been up to over the past few days…

"I am genuinely sorry for what I am about to tell you, but it had to be done. Yes, I did kill Nigel. I also took this walkie talkie. I couldn't have him contacting anyone and ruining my plan. I am afraid the CB radios in the village no longer work either. I have contacted the authorities and told them about Nigel Swanson and how he died; it was a deadly virus spreading the village that got him, and if they are to enter then many more people will die. I have organised supplies, but I will be the one who decides what is handed out. So, every couple of days, I will take my boat out to the edge of the river and pick them up. That way the outside World won't have to know what is going on." "Where did you get the boat?" I asked. "We've had it for years Sam. At the bottom of our garden. Now, I am going to give you some of these supplies, to hand out to people, so get yourselves home, and come back with Ronny's tractor so that you can load this food onto it. Say that you saw a police boat delivering it on the instruction of Nigel Swanson, who had contacted them before he perished. Say that this will continue until things are under control. That should be it for now. Except a little bit of information, I have for you. Now, Eddie was usually very careful with his investments, but not that clever. I think you should all know that the cash he invested for you is now in my name. As I mentioned to you at our last encounter; I found his accounts and his ledgers. After all, it was mine anyway, so I'm sure you won't mind."

"I need to know that people are scared. I need to know that they are going to be weak. I must be able to take everything from them and leave. If all goes to plan, then there will be no more deaths. There will be no more travesties over the weather either. You are all going to have to help me convince everyone that they should hand everything over to me. You have got a chance to change history forever. You could be the five people who ensure that the village of Danehill lives on longer than a year ending in '87 – for once. But just remember that I hold all the cards. I always will. I will kill you, your friends and your families. More innocent parishioners will perish. Don't ever forget that." I couldn't help myself. I too had a swing at Giles Smedley and punched him full in the face. I turned back to face the boys, and we all walked off seething.

We had to do exactly what he said, that was clear. So, we forgot the evening at the pub, and went back home to contact Ronny. We had a lot to discuss as we made our way home, and after a journey of soul searching, we concluded that it would be best if we told all. True, Giles Smedley said that he would bring devastation and death to all. But we thought that he was going to do that anyway. We couldn't trust him, he had already killed his own family, he had also bought vengeance against Sir Harry

Johnstone and the local copper. He was like a man possessed, and he wouldn't stop. We had to come clean. We also had no money left now, so maybe they would be more forgiving. Maybe they wouldn't.

We found Ronny and told him what we had been asked to do. He understood and took us there to pick up the supply run that Giles had collected. By the time we reached the village hall, there were very few villagers left. It was the early hours of the morning, and most people were now tucked up in bed at home. We helped take all the food from the tractor and stored it inside the kitchen. Once again, there was an atmosphere, we were aware that the following morning we were going to have to tell everybody what we knew. The reaction wouldn't be good, we knew that. We would get the blame for some of the deaths, I was nervous, and so were the other four lads. But we stood for something now, and we had the chance to save more lives than might be lost. The five of us had been on such a journey together. We reckoned that there was no way we could be beaten. We had been through so much. We had grown as people, and we had done it as a team. The five of us felt unstoppable, and telling all wouldn't end that. We had acted as one since the beginning of all of this, and we would continue to do so.

Monday November 9th

Pat was at the family home, helping his parents out at the kennels as usual. It had just gone 9am and he had a couple more hours before making his way down to the village hall. We had all planned to get there for 12 noon, as that was the time when most people would gather there for lunch. We wanted as many people as possible to be there when we broke the news about our robbery and, of course, all about Giles Smedley. Pat was alone, his parents and brother had gone to visit an elderly family friend who lived in the forest about a mile from the Wishing Kennels. Pat was busy sweeping and listening to his Sony Walkman, so he missed the sound of screeching tyres at the bottom of his gravel drive. He also failed to see the four tall demon like figures who got out of the van. Each one with an evil face that resembled Beelzebub. Poor Pat was listening to his cassette tape far too loud. It was only when one of the Helpers grabbed him from behind that he realised that something was amiss. But within ten seconds he had blacked out from the smell of Chloroform, which saturated the hankie that covered his nose and mouth. His Walkman smashed to the floor.

Rabbit, Carter, Seth and I patiently waited in the village hall car park. We were getting annoyed. Pat was always late, but it was one o'clock now. Surely, he hadn't got cold feet. That didn't seem like Pat at all. He was the brave one of the five of us. There was no way he'd back out. No, he was just late. "We can't do this without Pat" I said. "If he doesn't come then we'll have to respect his wishes. We can only do this if the five us are agreed on it." The others nodded in agreement. Giles Smedley then arrived on the scene. He was driving his dad Mercedes Benz and pulled into the car park and left the vehicle. "What, no Pat? I thought you'd all be here today for this big announcement." He said, "How on earth...." Said Rabbit. "Oh, I've got eyes and ears everywhere Rabbit. By the way. Pat sends his love." And with that he handed Rabbit an envelope, got back into the car and drove off. As he turned left on the steep bend to go down towards Chelforest he honked his horn and shouted out "I TOLD YOU BOYS. BUT YOU DIDN'T LISTEN, DID YOU? HAVEN'T I GIVEN YOU ENOUGH WARNINGS? NOW IT'S TIME TO LET THE FUN BEGIN." And then drove off at speed.

Rabbit opened the envelope and peered downwards at the contents. His face went very pale as he looked back up at us, "He's got Pat". He murmured softly and began to shake. In doing so he lost control and dropped what looked like some polaroid photographs to the ground. I picked them up. There were three photos in total. Each one of Pat with his hands and feet tied together and a handkerchief rolled-up and stuffed firmly into his mouth.

We couldn't say anything to anyone now. Giles had us over a barrel. We solemnly trudged back to Carters home for a debrief. We had no doubt that Giles had more dastardly plans for the locals, but we didn't know what. We knew we had to behave to save Pats life. Giles had proven that he would stop at nothing. We were all worried for the lives of our families. At least he hadn't killed Pat, but it was certainly a warning for us. I was first to speak "The only thing we can do is see what his next move is. We can't tell anybody about the burglary." We can't tell anybody about Pat either." Rabbit added. "His family are going to ask though, so we'll just have to say that he has gone camping or something. I can't think of anything else. There is now no way that he can leave the borders of the village. Seth, maybe you should also disappear for a while. We can say that you've accompanied him." Seth was on board with that. "Okay, good idea mate, but I'll keep slipping back to help when I can. If Pats relatives don't see me then we'll be okay. I could use the time to try and find out where he's hidden him. I might even be able to rescue the poor sod." Carter wasn't sure, "You can't mate, what if Smedley sees you, or even worse, gets you too. It might be best if you just lay low Seth. Then we can have a think about what we can do later." The only thing we could now do was sit. And wait.

Tuesday November 10th

I awoke around 9am the following day. I had a headache. I hadn't slept much at all. My head was full of thoughts. Concern for Pat, obviously, plus worry for my family and all the other villagers. I went downstairs where mum, dad and Sasha were sitting. We were able to use our aga but felt that we had to go to the village hall for breakfast. It seemed right to be together with everyone else in these difficult times. Mum was one of the few parishioners who could still cook at home and been tasked with providing food for others. We walked up our street laden with cakes and bread rolls. We arrived at the hall, and it was packed out with people. Even though it was November there was sunshine. It wasn't overly warm, but people were able to sit outside if they donned their jacket. This was handy as there were far too many locals onsite, and the village hall was already packed to the rafters with hungry visitors.

It was a good atmosphere considering the perils that had been put upon us all in recent months. People were enjoying each other's company once again and feasting noisily on the food provided. It was nice to hear people chatting, laughing and smiling again. We had been marooned on an island but there was a sense that we, as a district of willing people could still flourish and that all would be okay in the end. Young and old sat together, and there were smiles on faces again. But then a rather large spanner was thrust into the works...

The locals outside were busily tucking into their bacon and eggs, and gulping down their mugs of hot tea, when out of the blue everything completely changed. The air went extremely cold, almost freezing, and you could see your breath in the air as you opened your mouth, and the sudden noise of birds filled the air, and as we looked up to the sky. There were thousands of them all flying East to West above the hall. The noise was deafening. I had never seen so many of our feathered friends congregated on one flight path. It was scary. The birds had obviously been spooked by something, and this in turn was scaring the locals. There were crows, robins, black birds, pigeons, and all manner of species filling the air above our heads. The noise just wouldn't stop, and more and more people came outside to watch the extraordinary phenomena happening above us in the Sussex skies. Next the birds all moved across the airwaves at breakneck speed and down to the lower village and out of sight to the hinterlands below. And that was when the darkness arrived. It was like a sheet of blackness that followed the trajectory of the birds. It enveloped the village. It was only 9.30am but the whole of Danehill was covered in darkness. It was as though nighttime had decided that daylight was no longer needed. It had been bullied and pushed aside to make way for shade and obscurity. The whole of the village had transcended into total darkness. We had never seen anything like this in our lives. It was like a total eclipse.

People screamed and wailed, others sat in silence and shock, and others cried. People were shaking with fear. Everybody was beckoned into the village hall. There was panic. A freak occurrence had been bestowed upon us, and nobody knew why or what was happening. There wasn't much room left in the memorial hall as it was, but everybody obviously felt the need to feel safe and tried desperately to enter the supposed safety of the hall. Tables were pushed aside, and crockery and cutlery smashed to the floor, as room was made for the villagers from outside. As more and more people crammed in, there was less and less space available. People were being crushed by the sheer weight of numbers pushing their way through the throng, that was building by the second. Some tried to make room by scrambling up onto the stage at the far end of the hall, and more people did the same as space at the front of the hall became minimal. Suddenly there was a loud crash and the whole stage caved in.

It took a few moments for people to gauge what had occurred. A large cloud of quickly dust filled the air where the stage once stood. An almost unison of harsh coughing throats started to fill the air around us. Then people began to scream, but this time more in agony and pain than mystery and suspense. About fifty people had fallen into the large hole beneath the stage. It was obvious to Rabbit, Carter and I what had happened, and we prayed that the unlucky fallers were going to be okay. The villagers still above the huge gap immediately went into survival mode. People that could muster the energy were yanked free from the hole by the lucky ones still standing above. The many who had injured themselves in the fall were told to stay put. Luckily Doctor Lesley Turnbull was quickly on the scene to assist. A Dozen or so from the group had broken limbs, and it would take quite the rescue to get them free from the wreckage and bandaged up.

Other locals had noticed the ladder on the side of the deep hole and started to climb down to aid in the recovery of the wounded. There were children crying, there were people hyperventilating, and there were others who just stood there silenced; in shock at what had just happened. Once everything had died down, people starting to think on a more even keel. There was an immediate inquest. Some peered out into the darkness, checking their watches; had we really been here for twelve hours? No, it was still morning, according to their wrists. The whole event had happened so quickly but despite having no time to think, people seemed to engage in what was needed from them straightaway. At the far end of the hall, people were still being treated for injuries whilst others were engaged in conversation about the deep cavernous hole and the ladders within. It was not the time for this, but people were battling with bewilderment at the circumstances that we had been thrown into.

People assumed it must have been some sort of hideaway used during the Second World War. Villagers were suggesting that Phil Lomas would have known exactly what we had come across. The three of us lads knew differently. We knew exactly what it meant but had to keep it to ourselves. The complete darkness was something entirely different. We knew it had something to do with Smedley, but we weren't sure of his game just yet. Then as people sat around pondering the strange sight of darkness taking over our village, the whole event got even stranger...

That was when we heard the marching, the incessant sound of heavy boots crunching in unison on the road outside of where we had all congregated. It was so loud and sounded extremely close but as people looked from the windows, they couldn't see a thing. It was as if this echoing sound was right outside, but the blackness was darker than anything we had ever encountered before. If you looked out you couldn't see, even a centimetre in front of your face. Then the horrific moaning started. It was demonic, and evil, and it sounded like whoever was making this noise was in pain. There was a strong stench too – a horrific smell that nobody could place. Rabbit, Carter and I looked at each other. It was clear to us that this was the Helpers. Then as soon as it had started, it ceased to be. The light broke itself free from the dark, and shafts of sunlight once again streamed through the windows of the village hall. We ran over to check but could see nothing of the apparent creatures who had been marching towards us, and nothing of the darkness either. We expected to hear more steps marching away from the village hall but there was nothing. The birds had all returned to the trees and were whistling along happily as if nothing of any substance had occurred. A hurricane had swept through the village, then an earthquake followed by a terrific rainstorm, and now this. Nobody could quite believe what had been going on, but they were scared, petrified in fact. Giles Smedley and his gang of Helpers had begun their first phase of ruining and destroying the lives of the people of Danehill once again.

Wednesday November 11th

Confusion reigned within the perimeters of our now somewhat lost parish. A meeting was called, and it was decided that the best thing to do was to wait on the outside World to help us in our hour of need. The stocks were still coming in, although there was not a great deal. We still had many of the village farmers supplying wheat and grain and the families with non-electric ovens were doing their best to feed others in need. Those with allotments were doing their best to grow vegetables, and despite the bad weather they were managing to grow carrots, spinach and broad beans. It was clear that we wouldn't go hungry for a long while yet, it was a real team effort. Everybody else was convinced that a rescue would happen, and we would just have to be patient. The five of us, of course, knew differently. Rabbit, Carter and I were still separated from the other two, but we were hopeful that Seth had managed to track Pat down, and we were keeping an eye on what Giles and his Helpers had planned for him. We had instructed Seth to report back to us with any findings at regular intervals. But for now, the three of us were on our own. We went to visit Giles at his home, but he wasn't there. We needed information and wanted to see if we could strike a deal, but it looked like a last cause. His last words to us still bothered me greatly. "Now it's time to let the fun begin." He wasn't going to let this lie until he had more cash, more treasure, and more power over us all. We knew that if we told everyone what had been going on, that Pat would be killed, and so would our families. He had proved that he was capable of anything. All we could do was wait. It was like others were saying about our predicament; we just had to be patient.

That evening we decided to take a trip to the Alligator. It was quiet save for a few of the usual village drunks. Mickey Hamble was holding court at the bar, and everybody was being entertained by his stories. We had all heard them all so many times but that was half the fun, we all knew the punchlines, but he was always so drunk that he never remembered anything the next day. We had not caught any glimpses of the Helpers since the previous morning. We imagined that they either only came out at night, or they attacked when they bought their own darkness on the World. We assumed that they did all this on the orders of Giles, but it was all guess work. We just knew that at some point, they were going to cause havoc on us all. We decided that, if any of us saw anyone leave the pub on their own, then we would follow them at a safe distance just to make sure they got home in one piece. We stayed all night at the pub, trying to blend in with the fun and games, whilst also on guard. Mickey Hamble was the first to leave. I was tired, so we decided that I'd go with him, as I'd be going past his council flat on the way to my house. Christopher Wright was another local drinker, a funny man with a huge personality. He was big too so didn't need to protection in normal circumstances, but Rabbit kept an eye on Christopher as he too, stumbled down the main road home. Carter was still playing songs on the juke box, it was getting near last orders, and he was enjoying himself in the saloon bar, but he was also keeping a keen eye on who was next to leave. There were only a couple of people left who were solitary drinkers now. Carter assumed the others would be okay in pairs, so one person wouldn't get an escort. It wasn't a perfect plan, but it was the best we could muster at that time. The two that were left in the end were Tim Jarvis and Michael Dalglish. Michael lived in the opposite direction to Carter's homestead, but he left the Alligator next, and Carter had to follow. So, off he went, leaving Tim playing the fruit machine alone. Tim had recently come into some money. He was a betting man and had won big – he'd bet on a double at the US Open and Martina Navratilova and Ivan Lendl had come up trumps. Tim had won over twenty thousand pounds.

Tim left the pub about five minutes later and started the twenty-minute stroll back home. It was chilly, and he'd ventured two or three hundred yards down school lane by the time he realised that he'd forgotten his jacket. He'd go back to the pub tomorrow to pick it up he thought. Tim had drunk a few pints, but he wasn't what you'd call drunk, maybe just a bit tipsy. He'd recently visited the local hairdresser and been given a flat top, of which he was very proud. Tim felt that it complimented his glasses. He'd stop every few minutes and try to catch a glimpse of it in somebody's downstairs window. After a while, he could hear footsteps behind him. He turned around to see who it was but couldn't see anything. He thought he must have been imagining it so continued walking by himself in the dark. He got to number nine Oak Tree Cottages and decided to take another look at himself and his new hairdo in the windows reflection. As he tried to get himself into a good position to check he heard the footsteps again. He looked behind and then to his right, and to his left but could see no one. He lost his footing a bit and had to hold onto a garden gate to protect his balance. As he looked back up and into the window he could see his reflection perfectly. But beyond his spectacled face was another. Tim let out a yelp of surprise. The face behind him smiled, and he realised that this face was also wearing glasses and had a flat top. It also had the same ring in the left ear. It was Tim's exact double. "What do you want?" Tim shouted, but he got no reply. He started to run towards his home and safety, or so he thought. The 'person' followed him, without saying a word. "WHO ARE YOU?" Tim shouted again, petrified, his heart beating so loud and fast. "Leave me alone. I don't have any money" He ran up his garden path, grabbing at the keys in his pocket as he moved towards the door. He stumbled and fell onto the moist ground, his hand still in his pocket. The second Tim looked down at him quizzically. He grabbed Tim Jarvis by the lapels of his denim jacket and uttered the words "I am Tim Jarvis".

Thursday November 12th

Doctor Lesley Turnbull had been called down to the Jarvis home at 6am. Tim had been unearthed on the front lawn frothing at the mouth a couple of hours before. He'd been found by his parents. He was struck dumb, and his eyes were transfixed on something deep in the distance. He was staring straight ahead in fear, but they couldn't decipher what he was looking at. He looked straight through them all, as though they weren't in his vicinity. His look was vacant. His flat top had been completely shaved off, his earring ripped from his ear, leaving a horrible red bloody gash and a severe rip at the bottom of his ear lobe. His glasses were no more either and nowhere to be found. He lay upon the bed for several hours sweating profusely. Lesley was treating him, but without the necessary medicines there was not much he could do. His mum mopped at his brow with a cold flannel, trying her best to cool down her son. It wasn't life threatening, but it was obvious that he had been attacked and he was very scared of it being repeated. But there was more to the situation than that. Tim was losing his mind. Every so often he would shake violently, and his limbs would spontaneously fling out with great strength, it was a horrifying sight, and he had to be held down as he let out loud ugly screams of pain and terror. The news got round Danehill in rapid fashion. I met with the lads. We had done our bit and helped as many people as we could by watching over them as they wandered home. Tim was the unlucky one. It did make us think that maybe we were being watched. Maybe Giles Smedley was waiting for us to make our move before eventually making his own. Whatever had happened was certainly down to him. Within twenty-four hours Tim had been certified as mad.

Friday November 13th

Ted Brownlow owned the largest farm in the parish. A one-hundred-acre plot, it was called Sheffield Farm. Ted didn't work too much these days. He had turned the area into big business, offering cream teas, woodland walks, and a play area for the kids. He was making serious money from tourists. The animals had become something for visitors to gawp at rather than milk. But now he was having to be much more hands on and had been supplying the villagers with food and milk whilst the crisis still had hold of Danehill. He had also instructed his workers to build a bridge over the river, and the work was due to start soon. This would offer a way out for everyone if these peculiar things continued to happen. Brownlow had been a Godsend, and it was clear that Danehill were lucky to have him around. He did his usual delivery of stock to the village hall around 4pm and returned home to eat with his wife and three children. By the time they sat down to eat it was dark outside. His wife had lovingly prepared a meal on the aga, and he was looking forward to tucking into his steak and kidney pudding. As he took his first mouthful, he heard a tap at the kitchen window. Ted looked up from his supper and was astonished to see one of his cows standing there looking at them through the glass. "She's bloody got out" Ted said. "I'll have to go outside and get them back in the barn." His wife butted in "Take young Donny with you" she said. "Come on Donny lad" uttered Ted. "Let's go and tidy this mess up." Donny followed him. He wished he hadn't.

Ted opened the familiar door, the door he had opened out onto his courtyard a thousand times before. But what greeted him this time was extraordinary. The courtyard was probably about seventy-five metres square. It was usually empty save for a few tools, a barbecue and the family wellington boots. This time though it was full. Full of all his farmyard animals. One cow had popped up at the window, but there were now twenty of them all standing there staring at Ted and his son. There were seven pigs all grunting, there must have been about fifty chickens flapping their wings and making a racket. There was eight sheep and three horses. It was like a scene from the Animal Farm novel by George Orwell, Ted was almost expecting them to speak. "This is amazing" he said to his teenage son. "They have all come up to the house to have a look. We must have left the barn doors open, either that or we hadn't seen that the locks broke during the hurricane." His son nodded in agreement. "Shall we herd them up and get them back to bed then dad?" he asked. "Come on then lad." They were the last coherent words that Ted Brownlow would ever speak.

As Ted squeezed his way past the biggest of his horses he felt a nip on his ankle. He had been bitten by a sheep. It was nothing to him, as he'd been bitten many times before. Was he didn't expect was the reaction of the horse as he tried to push between the gelding and the house wall. The animal seemed to purposely push him against the brickwork and wouldn't move. Ted could feel himself getting crushed. His son could see what was going on so produced a stick to try and temper the horse and release his father. But this only riled the horse more. This also angered the rest of the animals, and they moved across to the side of the courtyard where Ted was stood. Another horse started to kick out at young Donny, and a cow bit down hard on his shoulder. There was a flurry of chicken wings flapping, as they leapt as high as they dared to take pecks at both males. Ted had almost lost consciousness and was sliding down the wall. His son couldn't speak, as he too was now being crushed by the sheer weight of the animals. Ted's wife and two daughters could hear the disturbing noises from outside and walked over to the window for a closer look. The scene that greeted their eyes was horrific. Both men in the family were lying on the floor covered in blood, being pecked at by chickens and kicked repeatedly in the head by the horses. His wife Doris screamed and as she did the animals all turned around and looked towards her "RUN!" she shouted at her daughters. And they all turned on their heels. It was too late, some of the animals were already butting and kicking at the back door of their home. They were going to get to the Brownlow family no matter what. Giles Smedley and some of the Helpers watched on from afar laughing at the scene ahead of them.

Saturday November 14th

The Brownlow family bodies weren't found until the Saturday afternoon. It was an awful discovery. A couple of the farm workers went on site and entered the courtyard. There were two human bodies outside, and they were surrounded by animals, some dead and some alive. The live animals were wide eyed and frothing at the mouth. It looked like the dead and ravaged animal carcases had been half eaten by the others. It was like a scene from a Zombie movie. There were three more bodies inside the house. The workers assumed that the five dead figures belonged to the Brownlow's but sadly the family were barely recognised as human beings anymore. Word got back to the village, and other farmers from the area were sent to the farm to dispose of the deranged farm animals. A local veterinary doctor had the opinion that the animals had gone through some sort of mental psychosis. They were destroyed immediately. Within hours of the vet and the farmhands leaving the property the place had been stripped bare of all its belongings. Giles Smedley's band of Helpers had helped themselves to the lot.

Monday November 17th

The following evening the two other lads and I went to meet Seth. We'd planned a reunion to see how he was getting on, and we were obviously keen to hear good news regarding the whereabouts of Pat. Seth had been camping on the edge of the forest and making frequent trips into the village under the cover of night. Seth really enjoyed this sort of thing. He was an outdoor type, and always thought of himself as a bit of a soldier. He had yet to locate our friend but had seen the Helpers marching through the area and believed it was only a matter of time until he found out where Pat had been put. We had bought him some extra blankets as the weather was getting very bleak. There was even talk that snow might be on the way. We'd met Seth near the old people's home of Saint Michaela's. It was an old mansion located right on the edge of the village and very few locals ventured out this way anymore. We assumed we wouldn't be spotted. We didn't want anyone knowing that Seth wasn't with Pat. Ironically, the only person we didn't mind seeing us was Giles, and within a few minutes of meeting Seth, Giles appeared out of nowhere. He was driving a range rover with a trailer on the back, it was full of Helpers. Giles pulled up alongside us "Good evening gentlemen. And what do you think you are doing out and about at this time of night?" he said as he climbed down from the driving seat. He shone his torchlight straight into our faces, blinding us for a while. He then shone the light into the trailer. This was the first time we had a chance to get a proper look at the horrible creatures he called his Helpers. They were ugly looking things, like how Satan himself is depicted in children's tales. They also had a ghostly look on their ugly faces, almost zombie like. They had talons for hands, and the smell was like nothing I had experienced in my life, and it was hard not to gag. It was like a mixture of sulphur, dampness and dog faeces. Indecipherable moans left their mouths. They were communicating but it was hard to understand. Some of it sounded English, whereas some of the language sounded like an old Latin language with a Sussex twang, it was all very odd. There was confusion on their faces. It reminded me of the look that a small child gives when they meet somebody for the first time, and don't know how they should act. They were breathing heavily, and you could see their breath in the winter air. They were under Giles' spell, that was clear. Most of them were bound together by chains, but there was a solitary figure right at the back whose head had fallen forward, it stayed very still. He looked more unoccupied than the others. Giles sensed us all looking at him. "Don't worry about that one" said Giles, "It's just had too much to drink." It wasn't that though, the Helper was dead, there was no breath coming from its mouth, it looked blue around its lips and its tongue protruded limply down the side of its chin. It did tell us one thing, and that was that the helpers were not invincible. This was a sure sign that they could be extinguished. "I think you are out searching for your friend. Well, you won't find him lads but don't worry. Pat will be returned to you unharmed once I have all that I yearn. This whole thing will be over soon. And then you might just be able to get back to your pitiful little lives." Giles turned away and got back into the Range Rover. "See you soon losers" he said as he drove off back down towards the main road. It was clear that we were all thinking the same thing "Those animals are beatable" I said. "Now we just have to find Pat, and we can end this whole sorry episode." We said our goodbyes to Seth and agreed to meet him again the following

Monday. Hopefully by then he would have located him, and we could bring a stop to Giles' reign of terror. Seth agreed to break cover and come and find us if he got news of Pat before Monday. Time was tight but there was now light at the end of the tunnel. We just had to hope and pray that nobody else's lives, or minds, would be lost before then.

Wednesday November 19th

Robert and Delia Frost lived on what was once Worsted Lane, which was the through road that connected us to the next village but now it was on the edge of the river that surrounded our village. If times were different, it would have pushed up the price of their house, as it now had river views. They owned a large property, with lots of land. It was a cold morning, and Robert was usually to be found in his office at his high-powered job in London but this island living meant he could no longer travel to the capital. He was working away on his computer when he heard a scream from the bathroom. He rushed across the long landing and found his wife in her dressing gown lying on the floor shaking and crying. The room was full of steam and vapour from the heat of the water running from the taps. Robert tried to get through to her "What is the matter darling?" he hollered. But she wouldn't - or couldn't answer. He turned to get his bearings to try and find out why and to what, his wife was reacting to like this. He looked in the bath that was still running, so he turned off the tap. There was no indication of her alarming state. He heard a squeaking sound and turned around to a message being written on the window. It slowly started to spell a short sentence. 'I S E E Y O U' Robert was worried, how the hell was this happening. He then heard a voice shouting out loud. 'I SEE YOU'. It got louder, 'I SEE YOU'. It got even louder 'I SEE YOU'. It got louder and louder which each cry of the words 'I SEE YOU' 'I SEE YOU' 'I SEE YOU'. Eventually Robert collapsed in a heap next to wife. A door slammed down in the lounge and Giles Smedley made his way up the stairs. He looked down at the startled faces of Delia and her husband. He'd contact Doctor Lesley Turnbull later and ask him to look in on the Frosts.

He knew that they would be the latest people to have the 'mad tag' placed upon them. He took count of his surroundings; he knew the Frosts were rich, but he didn't know that they had as many antiques in their home. This was a tidy haul. He smiled and left the building to continue with the rest of his day, and, of course, his evil wrongdoings.

Friday November 21st

Jeremy Clark was a well-respected and loved head teacher at the primary school in Danehill. He lived a fair way away from the village so had not been home since the hurricane. He had always felt a close bond with the people in the area and thought it only right that he stayed in the village to help since everything had started to unravel. He had been a regular at the village hall, eating his meals there and lending a hand. He had also been taking some of the children for impromptu lessons to stop them getting behind on their schoolwork. Mr Clark was in a unique position in that he held the deeds to the school building. During the second

World War many kids from places like London, Birmingham and the Northwest had been evacuees in the village, and Jeremy's older brother Brian was one of them. He had travelled down from Liverpool and had turned into an unlikely village hero when he saved the former school headmistress from certain death.

Brian had rescued her after a plane from the Luftwaffe had decided to drop its bombs over the village after a night of bombing England's capital. The German pilot needed to offload some weight to get back to Berlin, and he just happened to drop it right over the Danehill schools very location. The headmistress, Mrs Gallagher, was alone, marking homework in the classroom when the bomb hit, and Brian ran in and pulled her out from the rubble just before the roof fell on her. Brian was fifteen at the time, and a keen scholar. He was so moved by the reaction of the locals that he decided to stay on after the conflict and become a teacher, and eventually the headmaster himself. He did such sterling work that he was eventually given an MBE by Queen Elizabeth the second herself. He was honoured by the locals with the deeds to the school building. It was presented to him in the knowledge that he would never sell.

Sadly, Brian was tragically killed in a car crash in 1970, just days before his 45th birthday, and it was soon after that that Jeremy arrived to take over both Brians job and the school deeds. Jeremy was just as much loved as Brian, and, just eight years from retirement in 1987. With no offspring of his own he planned to hand the school over to the local council when he left his role, so that the local kids could still be taught and nurtured without the threat of the buildings being sold off for profit.

He was busily marking some extra-curricular papers in his office when he heard a door slam downstairs. Jeremy wondered down to see what was going on but could see nothing. He presumed that the wind must have got hold of the door and returned to his duties. Then he heard a window shut, and the glass shatter on to the floor of the classroom next to his office. Once again Mr Clark went to investigate, there was nobody there, but the window had smashed. There was glass everywhere, so Jeremy proceeded to clean up the mess. Suddenly, every window in the classroom started to smash open and shatter against the walls behind them. There was glass in his hair, and glass on the floor, cutting his shoe-less feet. There was blood running down the side of his face from the hundreds of tiny cuts on his slightly balding head. It was then that Mr Clark came face to face with three of Giles Smedley's Helpers. He was petrified. He was so scared that he was struck dumb. His body froze on the wooden floor. It was as though he was dead, but his eyes were wide open and very much alive. His breathing was quick, and his heart rate rapid.

Giles Smedley approached the headmaster and looked into his deep empty eyes. "I think Lesley Turnbull better get down to see you Headmaster. I think you might have lost it. We can't have mad people teaching the kids you know. We can't have mad people in charge of the deeds to the school buildings either Mr Clark. I think it's best that I take them from your drawer and look after them for safe keeping. If these were to get into the wrong hands, then who knows what will happen. Somebody might try and sell all this land. It must be worth a fortune." Smedley took the deeds. "You just lie there for a bit Jeremy, and I'll make sure the doctor comes and takes care of you." Smedley then proceeded to rifle through the personal belongings of Jeremy Clark.

Saturday November 22nd

Seth was struggling now. He had searched high and low for Pat but could find no trace of him. It wasn't an ideal situation to be in, and camping out in November wasn't easy, but he knew he was the best hope we had of finding our mate. He was an experienced camper and had all the proper kit. He had been frequenting an army surplus store in Brighton for a couple of years now. The owner had taken a shine to him and had phoned whenever he had any decent stuff in stock. He'd managed to keep the cold away with all his professional gear and had kept away from prying Danehill eyes. He found the search exhilarating. He had always fancied himself as a bit of a Rambo character, and he was acting up to this persona. Seth knew that he had to meet up with us in a couple of days and didn't want to let us down. More importantly, he didn't want to let Pat down, but he was running out of places to look. He had started to wonder whether Smedley had got rid of his mate already but didn't want to believe that. The thought of this made him very angry. He decided that he'd give it all he had for the next two days and ensure that he would deliver good news to his pals. There was a couple of areas that he still hadn't looked at, and off he went even more determined than ever to put a stop to Giles Smedley and his awful band of Helpers.

The church bells rang out, it was four o'clock, it was getting dark, and the cold was settling itself in for the night ahead. Seth was a country boy, and he could sense that a snowstorm was coming. He knew that he had to find Pat as soon as possible, if Pat was being kept in a place with no warmth to comfort him then he would be in big trouble soon. He trekked through the woods at the bottom of Oak Tree Cottages. There was good cover there, and nobody would chance being out in this weather or at this time. He dragged his tired body up the hill at the far side of the woods and reached the plateaux. Seth had a perfect view from here. He could see as far West as Pat's family home, the Wishing Kennels on Fanyard Lane, and the memorial hall, and the village centre to the North. It had been a long day, and it was time to set up camp for the night. He would be fine here, and it felt safe, he'd be okay lighting a fire, if he waited until later in the evening. He surveyed the vast area around him. His eyes caught a glimpse of a light down at the bottom Hollingford Lane. He took out his binoculars and viewed the scene below him. He could see an old farm building. The door was ajar, and a Helper was standing outside. Could this be the place where Pat was being held captive?

Sunday November 23rd

The snow started on the Sunday morning. It began around 3 o'clock and continued to come down heavily. By nine o'clock there must have been about six inches covering the ground. Giles Smedley had nothing to do with this, but it was undoubtedly in his favour. Snow on the ground meant less crops growing, and less food for the inhabitants of the island his powers had created. This was Mother Nature in her very prime, and in his sick mind he felt he owed the Lord for this. So, he got up and dressed in his fineries. Giles wanted to go to church to thank the Lord for aiding his sick plan over the people of Danehill.

The church was rammed to the rafters. There wasn't much to do since the storms, and people were ensuring they had as much contact with others as they could. The church was cold as the heating barely worked even during normal times, so now it was non-existent, the snow was still coming down outside. David Kendall, the vicar was seeing more and more people through his doors in recent weeks. This made him happy. His flock had gradually dwindled over the past few years. He was aware that visitors were here for the sense of familiarity, but he hoped that some might continue to drop in to his services once everything was back to normal. He was especially joyful to see Giles Smedley take a pew. He hadn't seen much of him since the death of his family, and he hoped that he could give him some hope and solace during the service. Peggy Long started up the organ and everybody stood to sing 'All things bright and beautiful'.

The sounds of the voices filled the air. There was a joyous feel to the rendition. People could come to the church and forget their woes. David Kendall had a huge grin on his face. He was a born-again priest. The hymn finished, and he took to the alter to read the Lord's Prayer. The congregation joined in, reciting every word. David then proceeded to start his sermon. He went to utter his opening words and then paused for a second. He looked up at the towering ceiling above himself and spoke "Why are you laughing?" The locals in front of him sat at their pews thinking this was some sort of dramatic start to a sermon, as he was known to do. But he asked the question again, this time shouting it out loud "WHY ARE YOU LAUGHING AT ME?" He looked angry. He looked annoyed and he looked confused. "STOP LAUGHING AT ME YOU BASTARD". The congregation looked concerned. They looked at each other in bewilderment. The vicar had sworn – and in church. He threw his bible to the floor and continued to look at the ceiling. His eyes looked wild and piercing. He screamed "WHY ARE YOU ALL HERE IN MY CHURCH?" David then bought his head down and bowed to all. He put his hands together as if he was about to pray. He then started to laugh. It wasn't just a giggle, it was a raucous, throw your head back wild guffaw. He didn't stop. He was like a man possessed. The villagers at the pews didn't know what to do. They looked at each other making faces, totally in shock at what was going on in front of their eyes. Eventually he fell to the floor. But he continued to laugh. He was holding his stomach in, as if he was worried that his tummy would burst open at the force of his laughter. A few residents moved down to the front of the church and tried to placate him. He threw his arms open and pulled somebody closer. He whispered in his ear. "Stop laughing at me". Then he stopped and stared at the ceiling once again. His eyes were like stone, and his breathing was weak, he had succumbed to the madness that had already taken in many villagers. Lesley Turnbull got out of his seat and approached the vicar. He summoned a few of the locals to sort a hand-made stretcher and David Kendall was taken out of the church and away to safety. Giles Smedley sat smiling smugly in his pew. He would now have access to Danehill Church, and all the fineries within. His power was growing by the day. The snow waged a storm outside, but the storm of madness that had gripped hold of the village, and its people, was more worrying. The congregation left the church, doubtful they would ever return with David Kendall at its helm. It was a truly sad day.

Monday November 24th

The snow was getting worse. It must have been about a foot deep now. Carter and I met up with Rabbit as we'd plan another meeting with Seth. Rabbit explained to us that he had had a visit from Giles last night. Smedley had asked for the keys to his BMW, and Rabbit said that there was nothing he could do, so now we had no car. Not that a vehicle was useful now as we couldn't leave the village unless we had a biplane or a sailing boat. It was obvious to us that our nemesis was flexing his muscles. He was telling us that he was in control of this whole situation and there was nothing we could do about it. We had to fight back somehow, and rescuing Pat was paramount in us showing him that we were not to be messed with either. The three of us were wrapped up warm with plastic bags inside our wellington boots to keep our feet dry. We left his family home, and we could hardly see in front of our faces. A blizzard had set in. The snow was hurting our faces as we battled our way across the playing fields. We were discussing the idea that the river may freeze if the weather continued to get colder. This would give the outside World access to Danehill, which, in turn, could mean the end of Smedley and his scheme but we had a way to go before then.

The three of us planned to catch up with Seth in the middle of the woods, near to our old primary school. We were to meet up by an old pine tree. It had red blotches of paint on it that looked like fire and blood, it would forever have 'The Dragon Tree' as its moniker. It had been named by local kids many generations back, and it was always a good meeting point. It felt safe, as did most places that involved fond memories of our youth. The blizzard was calming down now but our faces ached from the power of the snow filled pellets that had been showering down on us during our half mile walk down into the woods. The Dragon tree had an accustomed fragrance, even with the snow all around us we could still smell the familiar strong aroma of pine. As we approached, the sound of crisp snow underfoot changed to a spongey feeling. The splayed-out branches had protected the ground beneath the tree, so the snow hadn't completely covered the earth below.

There were thousands upon thousands of thin pine needles laying underneath. It was good to see that our tree had survived the hurricane, and Seth was sat there waiting patiently, and dry thanks to the security of the Dragon Trees branches…

"Alright lads" he said. "I hope you've bought me an extra sleeping bag, it's cold out here. Not that I'll need them for long now - You'll be pleased to know that I've found him". Seth laughed. We were so relieved. "Where is he?" Carter responded. "He's down by the sewerage works at the bottom of Hollingford Lane. They're keeping him in an old cow shed." Rabbit piped in, "What's the security like?" "There are a few of the Helpers around. But not many. I haven't seen Smedley yet. I'm not sure he even visits there. The only problem is that I have no idea how we ger rid of the Helpers. They are scary looking." "I know mate." I said, "They're not invincible though, we know that now. We saw a dead one, so they can be killed. Not that we are murderers, but we might just have to be if we want to end this war." Seth though, had a plan.

"Look, they might look evil, and dangerous, and they probably are, but they're stupid too. I have been watching them for a couple of days now. They are drawn to noise. Every bit of slight movement and they are off to see what is going on. They have been leaving the barn to check out cows when they moo. They've left the barn when they hear a car horn beep up the road. They're like sheep. Once one of them hears something, and heads off in that direction, then they all go and leave their post. I reckon all we need to do is get one of us to distract them whilst the others go in and grab Pat." We were enjoying this. Rabbit wasn't impressed. "That sounds far too easy" "I know" Seth replied. "There is one problem. I tested my theory last night. I got inside and saw Pat. He's okay, he was drinking a can of lager!" We all grinned. "He's chained up now. And the chains are connected to the stone wall inside the cow shed. We need the keys. And I reckon I know who has got them." I was adamant that Pat would be out of there as soon as possible. "Then we'll have to get them."

Tuesday November 25th

The following day Giles Smedley was on watch at the riverside. He had a few of his Helpers with him. They were hiding down deep in a ditch. Giles was surveying the river with a pair of binoculars. The snow had stopped now, so visibility was better, but the cold weather meant that the snow was still laying heavily on the ground. It was over a foot deep in some places. Making it very difficult to walk through some areas of the village. He scoped the river closely, taking in every part. He seemed happy that all was clear. As he put down his binoculars he noticed some movement in the woodland behind him. Lesley Turnbull came into view. He was out walking the family dog. "Hello Giles. How are you? Said the doctor. "Doc" said Giles. "I'm very good thanks. Just doing a. bit of bird watching." "I never knew you were an ornithologist, Giles." "It's a new thing Doc. I'm a bit bored, and just trying to keep my mind occupied until we get all this sorted." Lesley Turnbull looked beyond Giles' gaze, and into the direction of the river. "Keeping an eye out for boats too, are you?" he said. Giles turned quickly and put the binoculars back up to his eyes. "SHIT" he said. There was a police speed boat, it was manned by three or four officers of the law, and it had a large dinghy of supplies being pulled along behind it. The boat was about two hundred yards from the riverbank and was advancing at speed. Giles waved to the officers on board, and they responded with an elaborate salute.

The speed boat soon came to a stop, and the anchor was embedded into the deep mud on the riverbed. "Good morning" said the first policeman as he clambered ashore "We have got some supplies for you and your sick." "You shouldn't be here." Giles replied "We have all caught this virus. You are going to catch it if you come any closer." Lesley Turnbull was bemused "What vir…" he said. "Shut up Doc" Smedley interrupted him. He then put his fingers to his lips and whistled. It was a weird high-pitched noise. It sounded like a steam train. An ever stranger sounds then emanated from the ditch to Giles' left. That awful smell returned to the air, that marching sound now evident; Six of the Helpers rose from the ground within and marched towards the police boat. The police weren't quick enough to react, and they were soon being grabbed and pulled at. The helpers were far too strong for the officers, and they were punched, and head butted into submission. Giles then let out another whistle, even higher pitched than the last. And with that the policemen were held by their heads and put under the water and held there. Lesley Turnbull pleaded with Giles "What on earth are you doing? Stop them Giles, stop them. They are killing them." "Hush now Doc," said Smedley. "Hush". After a couple of minutes, the police officers' bodies stopped thrashing under the water, and there was silence. The Helpers had killed the police.

"I'm in charge now Doc. And you've witnessed my work. So, I'm afraid you are going to have to help me." Lesley Turnbull was petrified. "What, what, wha… are you talking about?" "I told you to hush Doc. Now I suggest you do as I say, or my helpers are going to have to harm you too. Now take this walkie talkie." Lesley Turnbull took the walkie talkie. "I want you to speak with the chief of police. You are a doctor. You must tell him that he shouldn't send anymore boats. Tell him that the virus has got worse. Tell him to leave all supplies on the other side of the riverbed, and that we will pick them up ourselves." "I can't." said Lesley. "Yes, you can Doc. Because if you don't then I will kill all your family and friends. And then I will kill you. You have seen what I am capable of. You are going to do exactly what I say from now on." Lesley Turnbull was shaking with fear, but he knew he had to pull himself together as he took hold of the walkie talkie and asked to speak with the man in charge.

Wednesday November 26th

Gail Sarsons lived in the village with her family. They all belonged to the house of scientology, so were looked at sceptically by the other villagers. People were wary of what they didn't have any knowledge of, so were guarded when it came to the Sarsons family. Her grandfather had created the Sarsons Malt Vinegar brand, so they were very rich indeed. They lived in a large house on Frishfield Lane, and the children had plenty of acres to play in. There were six kids in all, and Gail was the odd one out, the outcast of the family. Whilst her siblings played together every day, she was left on her own. From a young age she had had to get used to this, and so she had invented an imaginary friend by the name of Katherine.

Gail was now fourteen years old, but Katherine was still a mainstay in her life. Her brothers and sisters were having fun in the garden playing in the snow, building snowmen and throwing snowballs at each other. Gail was alone, as usual. Well, apart from her confidante Katherine, who was always somewhere in her vicinity. But nobody, of course, had ever actually seen Katherine. Gail seemed content though, she was making angels in the snow. And she was encouraging Katherine to do the same. Her brother looked over and saw two figures lying in the snow making pirouettes and star shapes. "Who is that with you?" Marcus said. His four siblings also noticed. "You can see her too? It's Katherine. We.re snow angels. Look." Marcus, Miranda, Alexia and Vincent were shocked. "Don't be silly Gail" Marcus said. "Who is that with you?" The other little girl sat upright, turned her head to the four and spoke "I'm Katherine and I'm real. I'm Katherine and I am Gail's best friend. I am Katherine, and I am here to kill you all." Gail's four brothers and sisters couldn't move; they were in shock. They were scared. Katherine then turned back to Gail. "Which one shall I kill first?" Gail didn't seem as scared as the others. "Don't be silly Katherine. Let's make snow angels." But Katherine wasn't interested in creating snow angels anymore. She wanted to hurt these five children. Giles Smedley peered over the hedge of the garden. "Hello children. I am sorry about Katherine, but she gets over excited in these situations. I have told her so many times not to be naughty, but she just won't listen." Katherine then stood up and screamed as loud as humanly possible, and then uttered a chilling sentence "YOU ARE ALL GOING TO DIE UNLESS YOU DO

AS I SAY." The five children nodded. Marcus wet himself as he stood, petrified at the thought of what this small evil demonic girl was going to do. Miranda started to cry. Then they all started to cry. They all curled up in balls in the freezing snow and wailed. They wailed for hours. Even when their parents took them inside and warmed them by the fire they wailed. Even when they were put to bed they continued to wail. They sent out word to Lesley Turnbull and he visited a very confused, concerned and solemn household. The doctor tried to help but this was beyond him and his expertise. He also had knowledge of what Giles Smedley, and his helpers were doing and couldn't say a word for fear of appraisals toward his own family.

Thursday November 27th

The following morning a meeting was called in the village hall. This was becoming a regular occurrence now. The Doctor Lesley Turnbull was leading the meeting and sat at the head of the table in the main part of the hall. People thought it odd that Giles

Smedley was sat next to him. Les put people's minds at rest by opening the meeting with the explanation that Giles wanted to assist in any way he could. He had felt lost since the death of his family and wanted to feel useful again. The whole of the onlookers clapped and cheered for Giles Smedley – apart from us three lads, obviously. Lesley Turnbull then addressed the crowd. "Ladies and Gentlemen. As many of you know, there has been a spate of strange goings on in the village in recent days. I have had to certify people as mad. It has been an horrific experience. I have known many of these people since birth and did not want it to go this far. But sadly, these people need help. As you all know, we are still getting very small packages of supplies from the outside World. So, to help these ill villagers it has been decided that the next run will see us hand them over to the care of the authorities. Luckily for us, the local council have agreed to let the families of the unwell also travel with them. They will not be alone, and they will be properly cared for. Soon, all will be back to normal, and we can continue to live our lives in Danehill to the fullest again.

I was fuming. I couldn't figure out what Giles was going to do with all these people, but it wouldn't be good. I also couldn't figure out what Lesley Turnbull was up to. Maybe he had been under pressure? Maybe he had been threatened too? Smedley was capable of anything. But what I did know was that if Giles was leaving to help move them then his house would be empty. This would provide us with the perfect opportunity to grab the keys and free Pat. The families of Robert and Delia Frost, Gail Sarsons, Tim Jarvis, and David Kendall were gathered in the village hall car park. Giles Smedley helped them all up the steps of his Range Rover. Some of them jumped into the trailer attached to the back and then they went off to meet their sick family members by the river and be escorted out by the Sussex River Police. This was our chance...

Seth was already waiting for us outside the former home. The property was on its last legs. It wouldn't be long before the whole place collapsed. Giles Smedley had continued to live here since the storm. It must have been so cold. One whole side of the property was exposed to the elements. The hurricane had ripped through the house and the collapsed chimney teetered worryingly on the first floor. You could still see inside from the road. It made us wonder just why Giles had stayed there. We were sure that somebody would have offered to have taken him in by now so there was obviously a reason as to why he slept and ate there still. We were going to enter to find the keys but maybe we would also find some clues to what he had planned next, and to why he remained living there. There was a chilled wind in the air, which whistled through the house. You could hear it blowing as we entered, like a boiling kettle. We didn't need a key to get in, as most of the windows had been blown in, and gave us easy access. Some of the snow had previously managed to lodge itself inside. It had now made huge puddles on the floor of the front toom and melted after Giles had lit the fire. We squelched our way into the kitchen and began to rummage through the draws to find the keys to Pats chains. We were quite relaxed, we had plenty of time. The escorting of the mental patients over the river would not be a quick job. We went over the whole kitchen and couldn't find a thing. Rabbit then went upstairs to check the bedrooms whilst Carter and I fought our way through the mess in the living room to look there. We must have been searching for two hours and still couldn't find what we wanted. We had turned the whole house upside down. It was no good, we hadn't found they keys. We would have to think of another way of releasing Pat. Then Carter looked out of the dining room window, across the snow covered back garden. At the far end was a bench, and lying on the bench was a Helper.

We approached the figure slowly, trying to keep quiet, which wasn't easy with half a foot of crisp snow beneath our feet. He was huge. His almost eight-foot frame couldn't fit on the bench, and his heavy legs protruded quite a way past the end of the wooden frame that held the bench up. Seth recognised it. "That's the one! That's the one who comes with Giles at feeding time. He's the one with the keys. He must have them". Down by his feet were four empty cans of local bitter. "He's pissed!" Carter exclaimed. He was right. The Helper had been drinking and looked comatose, but we still had to be careful. I reached down towards its pocket trying to make as least noise as possible so to not wake it up. The smell was unbearable, and I held my nose with one hand whilst the other entered its pocket and started to rummage inside. There were keys there, but I had to be careful not to wake it up. Rabbit leaned in "Don't worry Sam" he said. "It's not breathing. It's dead." Rabbit was right. The creature was no more. This made things a lot easier. "These things always seem to be either drunk or dead" I said. I grabbed the large selection of keys from its pocket, and we left the Smedley home. Now we had to make the long arduous walk down to the sewerage works and release Pat before Giles and the other helpers returned. The tide was beginning to turn back in our favour, and we felt confident as we made our way down to Hollingford Lane.

It was now two o'clock, and as we left for the Smedley house. Meanwhile, Giles Smedley, Lesley Turnbull and the effected were making their way to the giant river that now surrounded us. They were heading for the empty police boat that once belonged to the police officers that had been so callously killed just two days previously. It was meant to be a straightforward journey but the fact that the snow was still on the ground meant that driving was extremely tough. They had to abandon the four by four near the edge of the wood, and then take the last mile by foot. They reached the meeting point and then had to wait for the Helpers to bring the patients along. This wasn't an easy journey either, as the five ill villagers were not easy to control. The Helpers had them all chained up in a row but if one of them fell, then the others would follow. It was gone four o'clock, and was getting dark, by the time they were all together at the rendezvous spot. The families were so relieved to see their loved ones. But they were confused by the 'people' that had escorted them there. The Helpers were draped in a large fabric, so their demonic faces could not be seen. The people who had been certified as mad were tied and linked together with chains. Lesley Turnbull had already been instructed by Giles Smedley on what to say next. The doctor explained that the Helpers were nurses and were covered up so not pass on any viruses to the mentally ill. It was seen as the best way of getting them here safely. Of course, the families lapped that up. Although they were concerned about the chains. Giles told them that they all needed to be kept together in case they fell into the snow or the river. "Their safety is of great importance to us all, so I hope you understand that this is all for the best. Once we get them onto the boat things will be better." The families were thankful for the thought that had gone into both decisions. Giles then got everybody ready for the trip, "Ladies and Gentlemen. Please don't worry, any of you. This is going to be a good, and worthwhile journey for you and your families. The Doc will be driving the police speed boat over the river for you all to join on the other side. The ill amongst you will be taken into care, and the rest of you will be put in a hotel to wait whilst the treatment is undertaken. I am sure that Lesley will agree with me and put your minds at rest that all will be okay." Lesley Turnbull then spoke. He had a caring but authoritative voice that was hard to disagree with. He had the respect of the people of Danehill, so the families assumed they were in good hands. "Please don't worry everybody. We will all be back on dry land very soon. And then we can fix whatever ailments have affected you and your loved ones." Everybody smiled and nodded in agreement.

The speed boat could only sit ten people including the captain so the mentally ill would be the first to be taken across. Giles Smedley wished them luck. Lesley Turnbull knew he wouldn't be back. He knew that none of them would. He managed to keep a stiff upper lip as he boarded the police boat and started up the engine. He wanted to ensure that the ill knew nothing of what was to come. He waved forlornly to their families as the boat left the bank. They got about two hundred metres into the journey when

Giles Smedley pursed his lips and whistled. It was the same whistle they had heard before – the awful high-pitched sound that he used to call the Helpers. Next the horrible moaning sound and the stench of the creatures filled the air. It was so loud that it was impossible to even hear the speed boats engine. Fifteen of the Helpers then rose from the riverbed. They screamed a blood-curdling scream as they rose as one, taking hold of the boat and capsizing it in one swift movement. Robert and Delia Frost, Tim Jarvis, the Sarsons kids, Jeremy Clark, David Kendall, and Lesley Turnbull all perished at once, drowned by the cold icy water of the river that surrounded the village of Danehill. And then was a deafening silence, just for a moment, nobody could say a word. The families on the riverbank were in complete shock at what happened in front of their very eyes. They couldn't explain what had occurred. And they could not believe that their families were gone. The mothers screamed and cried. The fathers dropped to their knees in pain and the brothers and sisters of the dead collapsed to the ground. The horrific situation then got decidedly worse. A second piercing whistle from the lips of Giles Smedley indicated the second gruesome wave of attack. Five more Helpers stood up from within a ditch behind the grieving and confused families, who did not have time to think, or even ask Giles Smedley why he was doing this. The Helpers rampaged amongst them, using their long claws they ripped their bodies apart right there on the riverbank. These awful animals didn't move quick, but they moved amongst them with purpose. Blood curdling screams were all that the families could muster as they were ripped limb from limb by the Smedley hoard. Heads were torn off, arms and legs were scratched so that the veins underneath the skin was visible, and stomachs were burst open. Within a couple of minutes every single one of them was dead. All in all, Giles Smedley and his Helpers slaughtered twenty-three people that day. The edge of the river turned red from the pools of blood that flowed from the dead bodies. But it meant nothing to him. The only things he cared about was power and money. He knew that, with these families now dead, he could have all their belongings, their cash, and their homes. It was getting dark, and he jumped into his vehicle and turned to his demonic aides "Now let's go and finish those five little thieves and finish them off".

We were near the sewerage works by 3 o'clock. The four of us had found a good spot about fifty yards from the cowshed and were watching carefully what was going on at the site. There were a few tools leaning against the wall, an old petrol lawn mower was positioned by the entrance, and there were six Helpers there. Pat was inside under lock and key inside. But we had the key, and now we just needed to get in there and release him from his captors. We waited patiently until all six of the Helpers were inside. Seth then made his way down to the old farm building. He sidled his way along the stone wall and started to bang on the surface with a large garden spade. BANG, BANG, BANG. He was making one hell of a racket. Sure, enough all the Helpers made their way outside to check on the din. They caught a glimpse of Seth as he ran as fast as his legs could carry him. He took the most treacherous route up and over a hilly meadow that led to Fanyard Lane. His pursuers were awkward and laborious in the way they moved, and the tricky route made things even harder for them. They would never catch up with Seth. He continued to whistle and shout as he led them away like the Pied Piper of Hamlin. That was when Carter, Rabbit and I moved in on the cowshed. "Well, am I glad to see you." said Pat. We opened the locks of the chain and freed our pal. It was a relief, and we all hugged. Pat cried. He was struggling to move after a few days trapped in chains, so we held him up and moved him out of the farm building and across the fields on the opposite side to where Seth had led the Helpers away. Seth had circled back on himself by now. He was back at the cowshed. He then tied the lawn mower to a large pole and switched the engine on. It started up after a few goes and then sat there turning over loudly. The mower would now keep going round and round until the petrol ran out. This would attract the Helpers and Seth could follow our trail, leaving the Helpers very confused as to what had gone on. We were soon back at my house. It was empty. Seth would be with us soon. Pat started to tell us a bit about his time in captivity. He told us that his jailers could talk. "It's a child chat you have with them, as their vocabulary is not exactly adult, but they do talk. Some of it is English, but then they lapse into some weird Spanish or Italian or something" Pat mentions that they also talk in a very low whisper that is hard to hear. "I got friendly with one of them." He says, "It said that they don't hibernate like the witches. And they kill on the instructions of the witches. When the witches are asleep, they lay on the bottom of Worsted Lakes waiting for their call. I think that's what it said anyway!" Seth then arrived. "Hello mate, how are you? I've missed you." Pat and Seth hugged each other. This was great. We were all back together once again. "I'm just telling the lads about these dickhead Helpers. So, I got friendly with one of them and, after a while managed to convince him to buy me a few cans." We all laughed. This was Pat in a nutshell. He was being kept captive by a few demons and a mad man, but he still thought he had time to sink a few lagers. "I drank a couple of the cans, and then offered some to that thing but he refused. He got quite angry at the thought of it. He gave me a slap. So, I thought that's the end of that. No more beers for me. Anyway, I fell asleep eventually and woke up with a start. I had spilt some of my beer and my lap was wet. The shed floor wasn't level, and I noticed that a beer trail had reached the Helper on the other side of the room. It was lying on the floor licking at the puddle in front of it, like a man possessed." Rabbit joined in "Like an addict?" He asked. "Yes mate, and then he started groaning, his tongue got massive, too big for his mouth, he couldn't breathe, and he fell backwards. As dead as the proverbial Dodo."

Rabbit continued "Do you remember that letter we found?" We did. "It said in the scribblings that one of the Helpers had died because he had too much to drink." "And how about Giles" I piped in. "He only ever drinks wine. They're addicted to it. They're alcoholics, and they're allergic to ale." "Yes!" Carter butted in next "That Helper in the garden that we nabbed the keys from – drunk as a skunk, then dead. Then the captor, in the barn with Pat."

Rabbit had an idea. "Let's go to the Wagon and Ponies. I think we need to speak with Toggy."

Giles Smedley was not happy. He was not happy at all. He arrived at the sewerage works quite a while after we had left. He found six of his Helpers standing there transfixed, watching a lawn mower go round and round. Pat wasn't inside either. He was fuming. He had to come up with something, something that would bring the village together, and ensure that the five lads weren't going to get away with this. He called his Helpers to arms. "Tomorrow is our time. We will rise as one and kill them all. On my whistle at noon, I will call you, and you will come. And we shall end this war. In 1987 the prophecy shall continue, and the awful despicable little village of Danehill will be no more. It will be just like the old times, just like how it used to be. And I shall have it all."

Friday November 28th

Dad woke me up at around 11am. "Come on, up you get son. A meeting has been called. We must all be at the village hall for half past eleven. Apparently, there's some important news that needs sharing." Sasha butted in from her bedroom "Hopefully the council are getting all of this sorted, and we can get our lives back." "I wouldn't hold your breath Sasha" mum said. "What time did you get in Sam? We went to bed at midnight, and you were still out." "I can't remember" I said. "We were busy. And it was late, but I'll reveal all later." Mum wasn't impressed. "You do come out with some old rubbish you know. Okay, well you won't get away with this once school starts again. So, make the most of it."

As expected, the entire village turned up for the address. Just like before, the massive front doors had to be left open, so that the people that had to stand outside could see and hear what was going on. The car park was full of people, and the throng stretched back as far as the pub. There was a hum of excitement. Word had spread that we were meant to be hearing some good news about the river. Everyone imagined that our lives were going back to how they were before. It had been a tumultuous few months, that was evident to all, but the feeling now was that things were going to change. It was a crisp, bright, sunny winter morning and much of the snow had begun to melt as the sun shone brightly overhead. People were milling about from 11 o'clock in anticipation of the supposed good news. Coffee and tea were being served and there was a very relaxed and happy vibe. Children were running about, playing games, and friends and families chatted without a care in the World.

Inside the hall the meeting was being prepared. A long table was placed in front of the stage. The stage was still unusable since the accident and there were planks placed over the holes, that were trying their best to keep the area covered, and safe. Bright yellow police warning tape has been put around the area to keep the hall occupants away. Locals were enquiring about the smell in the hall though. There was a distinct whiff of beer in the air. It was pungent, and villagers were assuming that some youngsters had been partying in the village hall the previous evening. I was with mum when somebody commented on this, and she gave me one of her looks! Nobody knew who had called the meeting. People wrongly suspected that Lesley Turnbull was still in situ with the mentally ill, so he would not be in charge, a role he taken on since the untimely demise of Nigel Swanson. So, there was a big surprise when Giles Smedley manoeuvred his way to the front and asked for quiet. He had been assisting the doctor, but nobody thought he would be the one to speak in front of the whole of Danehill. However, the Danehillians just wanted to get in with it, and return to a peaceful way of living once more so just let him get on with it. Smedley stood up and began to speak...

"Ladies and Gentlemen of Danehill. Thank you so much for allowing me to stand here in front of you and address you on the goings on in the village. I have lived here my whole life and have always felt so welcome. The sense of camaraderie here is second to none." Everybody nodded in agreement. "As many of you know, my life was recently ripped apart when my family were killed during the hurricane." He wiped a fake tear from his eye. And then continued. "But the assistance I have had from many of you had been remarkable, so I just want to say thank you." He paused, the audience clapped and cheered, and there were tears in eyes. Giles then put his hands in the air to stop the noise. "That coming together has come to fruition once again in recent times, as we have had to cope with more horrible weather, a giant river encircling us, and people losing their minds. You have all coped admirably in such circumstances. You should all give yourselves a giant pat on the back." He started to applaud, and the crowd ahead of him did the same. The boys and I were fuming. We were stood together at the back of the hall. We couldn't work out where this speech was going but we knew that it wouldn't end well.

Giles Smedley continued with his speech. "I am happy to say that I have some good news for you all." Once again everybody cheered and smiled. "But before I commence with that, I have some sad information to share." The room fell silent. "The awful weather conditions meant that the travelling boat party with the ill villagers on board did not go well. The police boat they were in sadly capsized and drowned everyone on board." The room, and the car park outside fell silent. After a little while, whispers began and then started to become louder, and tears started to flow. This was a real shock to people, and a lot to take in. Giles read the room. "People of Danehill, don't be upset. We have lost so many villagers in recent times. But you must remember that life goes on. You must be strong." Smedley paused for approval but this time there was no cheers, no applause, no smiles. He had read the room wrongly. He looked happy. He had a wild grin on his face, that showed all his teeth. He looked like a mad man. "People, please be quiet. I have more to say, I have some news that is going to enlighten you all." But the people didn't quieten down. They needed time to take this all in. The loss of lives didn't mean a thing to Giles Smedley but everyone else there was human, and they felt the sadness and the awful sense of dread from so many deaths.

"SHUT UP, THE LOT OF YOU" Giles shouted. Now he had the room. People looked shocked. There was total silence now. We listened "You are all so weak! This village drives me mad. You get involved in everybody else's lives. You need to know all the gossip. You need to know everybody else's business. It is a horrible place to live. I don't know if you know or even care, but this village isn't meant to be. You are all meant to be dead now. You weren't supposed to survive the storm. I bought that storm down amongst you. I wanted you all dead." The crowd started to jeer, and shout. "Sit down you privileged little prat" shouted Doreen Coates' husband Gerry, Connor Bradford, Dad, Uncle Peter and Roy Braker shuffled forward, with a plan to grab Smedley, take him and throw him off the stage.

Giles then parted his arms out wide. He looked to the ceiling and shouted, "AND NOW I WILL END YOU ALL" An evil chilling laugh left his body, a wild laughter that shook the village hall to its core. Then he placed his fingers into his mouth and whistled. It was the same piercing whistle that some of us had heard before, and we knew what happened next. But this was a louder and more piercing whistle. It hurt people's ears. They were kneeling in pain on the floor covering their ear drums as the whistling got louder and louder. It went dark outside, once again the whole sky was filled with blackness. The dead of night was once more upon us. And then we got the marching. The sound of army boots en masse coming towards the Danehill Village Hall. It was threatening and scary, and nobody knew what to do. Confusion reigned inside and outside of the hall. And then they saw them. The figures that some of us had encountered before. But many hadn't, and they were horrified. The sound of groaning filled the air as nearly two hundred Helpers pushed their way through the crowd outside. That familiar smell filled the air, the horrid rancid aroma got inside the nostrils of everybody there. The smell of the beer mixed with the stench from the bodies of the Helpers was putrid. People were fainting all around us, there were tears and screams, and frightened children hid behind the legs of their mothers and fathers. Some of the bravest of the local men tried in vain to get to the stage, but there was no easy access. There were far too many panicking locals blocking their route. Giles Smedley stood watching the disarray before him. He had caused all of this and was loving it. He grinned. His face turned towards the five lads at the back of the room. We all grinned back. He looked confused by this. Why were they so happy? He thought, they were about to die. He was about to tell everybody they knew what they'd been up to. They would all be hated for a few seconds, and then they and all the other villagers would be no more. And they would all die thinking that this was all their fault. The five lads who had robbed him of his treasure, the five lads who had bought this on themselves. But Giles Smedley was in for a shock…

Then the Helpers entered our village hall. The locals froze with fear. They had experienced the darkness, and they had heard the noise, but they hadn't yet cast their eyes on these demonic beings that were now manoeuvring through way them all. They were in such close proximity that they could smell the stench of their breath. A few locals passed out at the sight of these large organisms who were moving at pace, their claws tense, their huge bodies bent over in anticipation of the death that they had been ordered to bring upon the Danehill villagers. People were cowering at the side of the large room, and some were in tears. How could things have got any worse? They had put up with so much, and now these beasts were amongst them. These beasts groaned and groaned. It was so loud, the windows started to shatter, and the people who were recoiling on the wings of the hall had to cover their heads, as shards of glass fell before them. Even the hardest of Danehill men could do nothing. They too were mesmerised by the power of these beings. And at the front, watching it all was Giles Smedley. He was enjoying the fright that he had put them under. He stood smugly smiling at the scene before him. "NOW MY BEAUTIFUL HELPERS. DO YOUR JOB AND TAKE DOWN THESE LESSER BEINGS. KILL THEM ALL MY BEAUTY'S. END THIS NOW" The first Helper to reach where Smedley was standing stared straight through him. It surged forward and broke through the police tape. Another one followed and his large awkward body knocked into Smedley, which caused him to lose his balance, he almost fell, he was in shock. More Helpers got to the front. They started desperately pulling at the planks that were covering the large gaping hole at the far end of the village hall. And then one by one, they started to lower themselves down into the hole. There were loud splashes as more and more of the Helpers joined their comrades in leaping into what seemed to be some sort of giant pool. The stench of beer grew stronger as the splashing grew wilder. They were swimming in the pool, a type of doggy paddle, and they were swallowing the liquid inside. They couldn't get enough of it.

Toggy stood with the five of us. We were still smiling smugly. Rabbit was a genius! The night before we had gone to the Wagon and Ponies. Toggy had sat down with us and heard our story. At first, he didn't believe the tale, but we soon convinced him. There was plenty of evidence; the storms, the darkness, the deaths, the people losing it – Toggy felt he had to take it all in, and credit us as truthful. If anything, he didn't see much of a future for the village if things continued like they were. He thought that he had nothing to lose. Surely something had to be done to help the locals and bring the village back to its former glory. We'd spent the night moving tonnes of ale from the pub to our current location. With the help of Ronny Braker, his tractor, and as much beer as Toggy and the pub could find we'd half-filled the deep hole in the village hall.

The Helpers were now helpless. The smell of the beer that engaged their tiny minds. Each one of them had succumbed to the alcohol. They had entered the hall on the promise of beer, and they would never get out again. Their bodies thrashed painfully about in the liquid; the ale was burning them, deep into their pores. Their pain was evident, as their awful groaning reached the piercing sounds of the whistles which Giles Smedley used to call them to command. It was like burning acid, hot steam rose from the lake of alcohol that had consumed their bodies. They and they blackened, and their bodies gradually disintegrated before our eyes. The stench was horrific; a mixture of faeces, burning and death. Within minutes all that was left was a pool of blood and guts, with the vapour of acid rising into the cavernous and now melting ceiling of the village hall.

Giles Smedley looked weak and disengaged. He was in shock. He lost his balance for a moment, and almost fell into the abyss behind him. He didn't have much left to say or do. He knew this was almost at an end. Everybody now knew it was him who had bought forth the perils onto the village. He used all the strength he could muster to stand tall. He addressed the crowd in front of him. "People of Danehill. Look at what has happened. We are ruined now. These awful creatures have taken everything from us. We must fight ba..." He was interrupted. Boos and Jeers filled the air. "Get down you evil bastard." "You're a murderer" "Shut up, and leave". He was never going to get away with it now. The Danehillians were a community that stuck together. People started pelting him with whatever they could put their hands on. They threw chairs, they threw food, they threw plates, "Murderer, murderer, murderer" they chanted.

Smedley looked drained. He looked despondent, and he looked on in shock. It was as though all the power had been drained from him. He looked a shell of his former, more confident self. He cut a forlorn figure, and he stood motionless on the stage taking in the atmosphere before him. How did it come to this? There were no answers. He had it all. And now it had all been taken away from him. There was no way he could come back from this. He was on his own now. No Helpers, no family or friends, and no power. The scourge of the crowd had weakened him. The community of

Danehill had destroyed him. The whole village had raised as one and Giles Smedley could take no more. He turned and looked at the mess in the hole below him. All his dreams were wasting away in the pool of predicament at his feet. He stepped calmly into the abyss underneath the broken stage. Giles Smedley was never seen again.

I looked to my right and smiled at Rabbit and Carter. I looked to my left and smiled at Pat and Seth. "Fancy a beer, lads" They did.

Monday February 1st

Thankfully, most things were now back to normal in the village. The river had been filled in, and thankfully we were no longer an island. The outside World came in to help us once more, and the Danehill community was back to its best. Many funerals and memorial services were held for the dead. People began to rebuild their lives. There were questions of course. We felt that we had to do something to provide some answers to our fellow villagers. So, Carter decided to make himself the new chairman of the Danehill Historical Society. He bought the letters we had found to the attention of the locals. This would give them some indication of what had happened, and why Giles Smedley had become the evil monster that we had all encountered. In early February, there was a big presentation in the village. The fact that there was new, evidence that Danehill was now officially part of the Domesday book made local news. The Mid Sussex Times newspaper ran a story, and a local television crew came onsite to interview Carter, as the new Chairman. He was presented with a large plaque, which was put in pride of place, ironically, on the wall above where the old collapsed stage once stood inside Danehill Village Memorial Hall.

Local governance decreed that the Smedley home should be knocked down. The house was connected to much terror and unpleasantness, and there was no way that anybody could live there again. Too many horrific memories blackened its image.

There would now be a memorial garden put in its place. It was a to be a peaceful haven now, and a garden where people could go and remember the dead, from 1987 and before. The diggers and the workmen moved in on a quiet Monday morning, and when they began to work on the excavation what they found was earth shattering. Beneath the house was a hole ten times deeper than the one underneath the village hall. It was filled to the brim with five hundred years-worth of treasure, money and antiques. Unsurprisingly all the Frost family antiques were also found, along with the deeds to the village primary school and many of the churches previous adornments. Tim's winnings, the Sarsons family heirlooms and the Brownlow farm ownership papers, and their belongings were also located. These were all returned to their rightful heirs.

The rest of the trove equalled to millions and millions of pounds that could be used to rebuild our village. There were now no more Helpers, no more Giles Smedley and no more witches. And nobody would ever get to find out what us five ordinary Sussex lads had done on that Saturday night in June of 1987.

The small village of Danehill could thrive once more; and in a year that ended in eighty-eight!

The End.

Printed in Great Britain
by Amazon